I removed my tie and placed it on the small desk, then I hung my suit jacket on the hook by the closet, and turned on the table lamp. Lizzie emerged minutes later clothed in nothing but her undergarments. She slid over to me and wrapped her arms around my neck. Then she kissed me. It was a soft kiss. A kind kiss. An inviting kiss.

She pulled back and smiled.

I put my hands on her hips. They were nice hips, soft and curvy, just like hips ought to be. They were inviting me as well. Inviting me to do things I had no business doing with someone I had no business being with. But there she was, standing in front of me, fiddling with my tie, wearing next to nothing, with perfect red lips, staring into my eyes. I pulled her head to my chest and she hugged me tightly.

ROSSI'S GAMBLE

A Max Rosssi Crime Noir

by

Paul W. Papa

ROSSI'S GAMBLE
Published by HPD Publishing
Las Vegas, NV 89105

Published in the United States by:
HPD Publishing (A division of STACGroup llc)
PO Box 230093
Las Vegas, NV 89105

ISBN (pbk): 978-1-953482-00-6; (10-digit) 1-953482-00-7
ISBN (ebk): 978-1-7344057-9-8; (10-digit) 1-7344057-9-1

Cover design by darngoodcovers.com
Cover Model: Pinup Model and Burlesque Performer Bebe Caliberr Mercy
Cover Photo: Dev Pagan-Perez

Keep up with Paul W. Papa's books at https://mailchi.mp/8be9ac154607/paulwpapa or https://paulwpapa.com/

8 10 6 9 1 5 2 3 7 6

For Melissa.

ROSSI'S GAMBLE

ONE

BABYSITTING. YOU CAN call it what you want, but I call it babysitting. Only the babe was a five-foot, four-inch, blonde dish in a deep-blue sheath tulip dress with a matching hat and three-inch heels. I was assigned to her by my new boss Frank Abbandandolo, who went by the moniker "Fingers," on account of his nimbleness, as a kid, at relieving people of their valuables. It was an activity he had long since abandoned, though he had found others to take its place. Fingers was New York mob tried and true. He probably bled marinara sauce. He ran things at the Sands Hotel and Casino. Not so much the day-to-day affairs, more the extracurricular activities. He became my boss when I took the position as a private dick. I needed the cash and the offer was too good to refuse. So I didn't.

I didn't have a problem working for mobsters, though I wasn't one myself. I had tried the life of course—my father was in it after all—but it didn't suit me. The benefits were high, but the life expectancy was low, and there was no retirement. Well, except for the stone garden, of course. But who wanted that? So, while I agreed to work for gangsters, there were stipulations to my employment. I wouldn't do anything illegal, and I didn't want to be tied to the Sands completely. Fingers was amiable to my conditions, so we struck an accord.

My current assignment was playing escort to Elizabeth Averill; a woman who preferred to be called Lizzie, or so she said. She was with the Sands' current whale—a name they give to anyone who comes into the joint with pockets full of cabbage ready to lay it on the tables. Lizzie was the girlfriend, and when watching her man gamble grew tiresome, she needed a diversion. Whales are treated like kings, and when the king's girl needs some entertainment, the court jester gets called.

"We need to get her out of here," Fingers said. "She's affecting his game."

"So I'm to be her kidnapper?" I asked.

"I prefer 'escort,'" he countered. "Besides, she asked for you specifically."

Lizzie and I had just come from the El Portal Theatre on Fremont Street, where we took in an upbeat flick called *The Land of the Pharaohs*, starring Jack Hawkins, Joan Collins, and Dewey Martin. It was Lizzie's pick. After all, she was the king's queen. Personally, I could take it or leave it, though Joan Collins' two-piece was certainly worth the price of admission.

My companion hooked her arm in mine as we made our way down the sidewalk to no place in particular. Every town had a main drag; a place where business is conducted and people gather. Downtown. The lifeblood. The heart of the city. In Las Vegas, that was Fremont Street.

The street was the first in town to have a brick

building, and it was the only place where all the buildings intentionally faced the street. That brick building was the Nevada Hotel, built in 1906, just a year after the town's founding. Fremont Street housed the pharmacy, the bakery, clothing stores, hairdressers, jewelry stores, and the movie theater. Recently, however, much of the downtown area had been taken over by gambling halls. It changed the skyline and it changed the town.

Lizzie didn't seem to mind. She was happy just being out in the sun. Lizzie was one of those gals men wanted to be near. She had ice-blue eyes, a perky nose, olive skin, and wavy hair that I suspected came from a bottle. She was pretty—the kind of pretty that doesn't hold with age.

"Tell me about yourself," she said as she patted my arm. There was a bit of a skip in her step, like a young girl on her first date.

"What's there to tell?" I asked.

She let out a puff of air. "Everything. Where are you from? Why are you here in Las Vegas? What do you do for fun? You know, the usual bingo."

"What, are you writing a book?"

"No, silly," she said and slapped my arm. "I'm just trying to get to know you. If we're going to be spending time together, I like to know who I'm with."

I was beginning to rethink my career choice. "I'm from Boston," I said. "I came here for a bachelor party and never left, and I'm not allowed to have fun. Mother's orders."

That brought out a smile. It was a pleasant smile; one that fit well on her face.

"That's better," she said. "Now ask me about me."

"Where are you from?" I asked. "Why are you here in Las Vegas? What do you do for fun? You know, the usual bingo."

PAUL W. PAPA

That got me another slap.

"I'm from California," she said. "LA area. I came here with Richard on a lark. He had money and I had time."

"So you're making time with him then?" I asked.

It was an ill-mannered question, but that didn't stop me. She should have slapped my face, but she didn't, so I asked another. "I suppose you're an actress?"

"Naw, those dames are a dime a dozen," she said. "Though I do like the movies. What did you think of the picture?"

I made an unpleasant noise. "I would have preferred Mister. Roberts," I said. "Fonda, Cagney, and Powell—how can you go wrong?"

"That's such a 'guy' response."

"Well, if the shoe fits, scarpe diem, I say."

That got me a wrinkled forehead. I preferred the smile.

"Scarpe is Italian for shoes," I explained.

"I don't get it," she said.

I assured her there wasn't much to get. We continued on. After a minute, she stopped and stepped in front of me. She placed both hands under my lapels and somehow managed to raise herself even higher than her heels seemed to allow.

"You're kind of cute," she said.

"My mother would agree," I confirmed.

"You're clever," she added. "I like that."

What was I to say?

She ran her fingers up and down my lapels, then placed her palms on my chest. Her eyes met mine, then continued downward, stopping at my mouth. "You're the kinda guy a girl could fall for," she said.

"You mean like Richard Dorsey?"

"Who?" she asked, keeping her eyes where she'd left them.

"Richard Dorsey," I repeated. "Your boyfriend?"

"Oh, he's not my boyfriend," she said. "He's just my entertainment."

"You're kind of a fickle gal, aren't you?" I asked.

She returned to my eyes. "I'm a gal who knows what she wants," she said. "Now, kiss me."

It was not a request I had anticipated. "Right out here?" I asked. "In the open, in front of God and the whole world?"

"Uh-huh."

"I don't think that's such a good..."

"Oh, pish posh," she said, cutting me off. And before I could counter, she did the deed herself. Her lips were soft, but firm, the kind of lips a guy could get used to. I had no choice but to return the favor.

When she was done, she pulled back and ran her pointer slowly across her lips, like she was wiping off milk, or possibly melted chocolate. "That was nice," she said, then returned to her spot beside me and hooked my arm again.

I walked a little lighter in my scarpe.

We were just about to pass MJ Christensen Jewelers when Lizzie stopped us. "Let's go inside," she said. "You can pretend I'm your girl and you want to buy me something."

I rolled my eyes.

"C 'mon," she said and pulled me inside.

We passed the security guard standing, arms folded, in the corner and headed straight to the counter where we were met by a fine-looking gentleman in a twist-woven, single-breasted, eggplant-colored gabardine suit with matching slacks. He had a demure tie and a matching square. "May I help you?" he asked.

"Oh, Maxie," Lizzie began, "Do you really want to buy me a bracelet?" she said, feigning excitement. If she wasn't an actress, you could have fooled me.

I didn't know what to do. "Sure, Sweetie," I said clumsily. "Anything for you."

We walked over to the counter housing the bracelets and the gabardine suit pulled several out for us to see. I placed my lid on the counter next to them. Marcus Joy, the "MJ" of MJ Christensen, was sitting in a back room, revealed by a small sliding glass window, in front of a placard that bore his name. He had on those glasses watch repairmen wear, which was fitting because he had a watch in his left hand and some type of small tool in his right. He gave us a raised brow.

The first thing the gabardine suit showed us was a Cartier panther head piece that would have fit right smartly on Joan Collins' wrist. It was yellow gold with emerald eyes and a diamond-encrusted head. The price tag was north of two Gs. Lizzie tried it on. I gave a loud whistle.

"Is there a problem, sir?" the gabardine asked with a sufficient amount of disdain.

"How about we keep it under the cost of a small country," I suggested.

"Oh, Maxie," Lizzie said. "Don't be a wet rag."

"Perhaps this would be more to your liking," the gabardine suit said. He pulled out a Lavencious tennis bracelet and slid it onto Lizzie's eager wrist.

"It's simply gorgeous!" Lizzie said. "What do you think, Maxie?"

I assured her it was stunning but was beginning to find the game tiresome. "Hurry, my dear, or we'll be late for dinner," I said, channeling Powell. "Perhaps we should come back another time."

"How about pearls?" Lizzie said to the gabardine suit. "Do you have any pearls?"

"Certainly," he said. "I have a fine piece right here."

"Grace Kelly wears pearls," Lizzie said to me.

"Yippie, skippie," I offered.

Her eyes rolled. The gabardine suit placed the pearls on Lizzie's wrist next to the tennis piece. "Which do you prefer, Maxie?" she asked.

"I prefer being on time," I told her.

"You're impossible!" Lizzie exclaimed. She pulled off the bracelets and headed with a huff for the door, bumping me on her way. The security guard opened it quickly as she stormed out. I looked to the gabardine suit, he had nothing to offer, so I picked up my lid and turned to leave myself.

"Excuse me," the gabardine suit said. "I'm going to need the panther head back."

"What are you talking about?" I asked.

"The Cartier panther head bracelet," he said. "I'm going to need it back."

MJ looked up from his window. Security stepped behind me.

"I don't have the panther head," I said. "Look, this was all a lark. Just for fun. She's not my girl and I never intended to buy her anything. I'm sorry we've wasted your time, but I don't have your bracelet."

I turned again to leave, but security came up behind me and pinned my arms back. I tried to pull away, but the brute was stronger than he looked and he had me good. The gabardine suit came out from behind the counter and began fishing in my pockets.

"Get your hands off me!" I yelled just as he pulled a yellow gold panther head bracelet with emerald eyes and a diamond-encrusted head from my right jacket pocket.

He held it up in front of me. "Call the police," he said.

TWO

THREE HOURS LATER, I was sitting in a jail cell weighing my options. There wasn't much to weigh. I'd been set up with no way to prove it. My alibi hadn't stuck around and the police were all too willing to believe the gabardine suit over me. It didn't matter that no harm had actually been done; it was the thought that counted.

I was also left to wonder as to Lizzie's motives. If it truly was just a lark, why hadn't she just come back into the store and explained it all? Oh no, when she left, she left for good—leaving me high and dry, holding the bag, along with a nice charge of larceny and burglary to top it off. Now here I was, behind bars, next to a scared kid trying to look tough in a leather jacket and cuffed dungarees, and the town drunk in a wrinkled suit sprawled across the only bench.

It was at just that moment that a giant of an Irishman came strolling by. A detective by the name of Lieutenant Connor McQueeney, "Queeney" to those who knew him.

He wore gray slacks and a white shirt, the sleeves rolled up to his elbows. His tie was loosened and his top button undone. He must have caught me out of the corner of his eye because he did a double take that would have snapped the neck of a lesser man. Like me, Queeney was a transplant from Boston, and, like me, he came here to get away from the family. Only his family were all blue bloods, though the blue didn't always run true.

"Well, if it isn't Max Rossi," he said in his Boston-Irish brogue. Queeney looked down at me with judgmental eyes. "It's nice to see you in the can. Bars are a good look on you, I only wish I'd 'a been the one who put you there."

It was nice to see a friendly face.

"Don't be disappointed," I said. "We can't always get what we want, now can we?"

"Oh, I'm not disappointed," Queeney countered, his grin filling his ruddy mug. "I'll take it any way I can get it. Even if it's someone else's collar."

"I'm glad I could brighten your day."

"So," he said, "what're you in for?"

"Larceny, with a burglary chaser, only I'm innocent."

Queeney let out a sharp snort. "That's what they all say."

"I imagine they do," I countered. "Only in my case, it's true."

"You don't say."

I stood and walked over to the bars. "In fact, I do say."

"And I suppose this too is some dame's fault."

He had me there. I flashed a sheepish grin.

Queeney gave me the once over. "Why haven't you posted bond?"

I pulled out the linings of my pockets. I think I saw

moths fly out.

"So call one of your trouble boys at the Sands."

"I doubt my employers would be pleased with my present predicament," I told him. "I was hoping to keep it under wraps for the time being."

That got me another snort. "Good luck with that," he said.

"I don't suppose there's anything you can do to help me along?" I didn't think there was, but it didn't hurt to ask. My only other option, as Queeney pointed out, was to call Fingers, but it wasn't an option I was eager to pursue.

He stood there for a moment, letting the notion rattle around in his skull like a pinball. I let it play out.

"Think you can keep your nose clean?" he finally asked.

I promised to shower every day. Then added, "Scout's honor," while holding up fingers in what I hoped resembled the Boy Scout's Promise. What did I know? There were no scouts in my neighborhood. Unless you counted the lookout for the hubcap boys.

"I'll see what I can do," he said. An hour later I left the clubhouse, headed, via scarpe, to pick up my Roadmaster. It was exactly where I left it on Fremont Street, but there was a new decoration on the windshield, tucked neatly under the wiper blade. Greetings from the City of Las Vegas in the form of a parking citation. I was having a day.

I folded the citation, slid it into my breast pocket, and brought the car to life. The tires squealed as I yanked it out of the parking space. I may have gone a little heavy on the gas, but I had a bone to pick with Miss Elizabeth Averill and I was pretty sure I knew where she'd be.

THREE

I PULLED INTO the porte cochère, hopped out, and flipped a nugget to the valet. I was a man on a mission. I pushed through the front doors of my new digs—well, my new employment digs anyway, like I owned the place, tipping the doorman as I passed. Walking into the Sands was like walking into the middle of a party going gangbusters: music was playing, drinks were being served and women were squealing with delight at the sounds of coins dropping into metal trays. The joint, as the kids say, was jumpin'.

I stood a minute and let my eyes adjust to the relative darkness. Casinos were interesting places. Every detail was intended to keep customers focused on the slot machines or table games. The carpet was busy, forcing the eye upward. There were no windows or clocks in the place, no way to determine time—current or spent. Lights were lowered, but not too much. Just enough to provide that party atmosphere. You had to hand it to the guy who figured it all out because it worked like a charm.

I'd only made it a few steps into the place when I was approached by a young bellhop in a pillbox hat that was intentionally too small for his head and a faux military-style uniform with enough gold buttons for the entire Chinese army. A stripe on each leg helped him find his pockets.

"Mr. Rossi," he said. "Mr. Abbandandolo would like to see you."

That couldn't be good.

"He asked me to tell you, as soon as you arrived, to meet him in his office on the mezzanine."

I thanked the kid, handed him a dime, and headed to the stairs leading up to the mezzanine, which was simply a fancy name for the second floor. Unlike the casino downstairs, the offices were all business. This was where the people who ran the place hid out when they weren't on the casino floor. The size of the office let people know your position in the hierarchy. Jake Freedman had the biggest, he was the president after all. Well, the president on paper anyway. Freedman may have run the day-to-day activities, but it was Meyer Lansky who really ran the joint, with the help of Fingers, of course, and the rest of the New York outfit.

The entrance to Finger's office was guarded by a doll named Leona, who resembled Vivien Leigh in the right light and Veronica Lake from the neck down. She wore a tight green turtleneck sweater over her Maidenform and a matching pencil skirt. It was the best thing I had seen all day. Leona was busy working the keys of a typewriter when I approached her with my best smile.

"When are you going to leave this life and run away with me?" I asked.

"Oh, no," she said, looking over her cat-eye spectacles

at me. "I know your kind. Love 'em and leave 'em is your game."

"But I could change for you," I promised.

"Leopards don't change their spots," she chided.

She was probably right.

Leona picked up the receiver and pushed a button on the phone. "Mr. Rossi is here to see you," she said, then put the phone down. "You may go in."

"Last chance," I said.

"Hmmm," she said through pursed lips. "I'll pass." She offered to get me a drink and I ordered a manhattan with rye. It was probably too early to drink, but I had been hardened by my time in the joint, so I threw caution to the wind.

Finger's office looked nothing like the casino below. The walls were covered in light-brown wood panels and the floor in tightly woven, golden-fiber carpet. His desk was modern minimalistic, sturdy without being extravagant. Leona followed me inside and headed to the wet bar that rested against one wall.

Fingers was sitting at a set of table and chairs near the window, but he wasn't alone. That didn't help my blood pressure any.

"Max, come in," Fingers said. He stood and extended his hand.

I took it.

"Please," he said. "Have a seat."

I removed my lid, set it on the table, unbuttoned my coat, and did as I was told, choosing the chair that had been pulled out from the table in anticipation of my arrival.

I looked at the third man. He didn't smile, so I didn't either. I knew who he was, of course, but I waited like a good boy for the introduction.

Fingers sat down as well. He was dressed in a loose white shirt and Cutter Cravat tie. His tent of a suit coat was resting on a rack to the rear of his desk. He picked up a stogie from the ashtray in front of him and waited for Leona to bring me my drink. Fingers was a man who should never be allowed to smoke a cigar. He just didn't do it right, leaving it in his mouth too long and biting down too hard on the end, creating a mush of a mess that was difficult to look at, never mind smoke.

"Here you go, Mr. Rossi," Leona said. "A manhattan with rye."

I thanked her and waited as the two men watched her leave. When the office door closed, Fingers spoke.

"You know Mr. Lansky?" he asked.

"Of course," I said and reached out my hand. Lansky took it. He was a diminutive man. Then again, Fingers could make even Jumbo look small if he was sitting in the chair next to him. Still, Lansky struck me as a man who'd have trouble buying clothes off the rack. But what did I know? Lansky was one of those guys born with a 50-year-old mug. If it wasn't for his height, he could have been served in any bar when he was three, maybe four. He probably started smoking at five.

What he lacked in stature, though, he made up for in power. Lansky was Jewish Mob but was also buddies with Salvatore Lucania, who went by Charles "Lucky" Luciano, of the New York Lucianos. Founding member of Murder, Incorporated. Meyer was born Maier Suchowljansky, but somewhere along the line he changed the spelling of his given name and shortened his surname. I could see why. He was also a friend of my father's.

"I heard you got pinched this morning," Lansky said. A deck of Luckys rested on the table in front of him. One was missing.

"A case of mistaken identity," I assured him.

His face grew stern. He tapped the ashes from the end of his smoke into the joint ashtray positioned between the two men. "I don't like trouble," he said.

"It was a simple misunderstanding," I offered. "Easily resolved."

"Good," Lansky said. "'Cause I have a job for you."

I raised an eyebrow.

"Don't worry," he said. "Fingers told me your conditions. It's a legitimate job."

I looked to Fingers. He nodded.

"The Highwaymen are in town and I need you to stop them," Lansky continued.

"Highwaymen?" I asked.

He took a puff of his cigarette, then blew the smoke into the air. "A group of cheaters and con artists."

There were three things that would get you into trouble in a casino—especially a mob-run casino. Three things that would raise a red flag. Three things you can never do. The first is to mess with the casino's money. You mess with the money and it isn't going to go well for you. You'll find yourself missing an appendage. One you like. One you're attached to. One of which you may have grown fond. Not a big toe or anything like that. Something more substantial. Something meaningful. That is, if you don't find yourself out in the desert. Digging yourself a hole. A .38 pointed at your head. The second thing you don't mess with in a casino is money. You never mess with a casino's money. I'm betting you can guess the third.

"Why do you need me?" I asked. "Don't you have a way of dealing with cheaters?"

Lansky tried a smile. It didn't suit him. "We got a good thing going on here, Rossi, and we're not looking to mess that up. Sure, we could take out a player, try to set an example, but that would shine an unwanted light on things and who wants that? The Highwaymen are like a den of vipers and like any snake, you need to cut it off at the head, so it doesn't bite you back."

Lansky said some other words, but I didn't really hear them. As they shot past my ears, I began to focus on the man's tie bar. It was silver and housed a perfectly round stone that looked very much like an onyx. It was inlaid with four fleurs de lis, forming a cross. A speck of light from the ceiling glistened near the edge of the gemstone, which was polished to a high shine. I recognized the stone because my grandmother used to have one just like it in a setting she wore on her finger. My Nona, who was half a gypsy, once told me onyx had healing properties, and that a person should always have one in their possession. I found it interesting that this man, this mobster, who had little qualms about taking life, had chosen a healing stone as an accessory. I wondered if he knew.

I heard Fingers speak. "You still with us?" he asked, distantly.

I knew what I was being asked. A line drawn in the sand. A block knocked off my shoulder.

"So you want me to put the finger on the head," I said.

Lansky pointed at me with his two digits and his smoke. "Smart kid," he said. "Fingers was right about you."

Who was I to argue?

"You're gonna need to go undercover on this one, Max." Fingers added. "You'll need to find them, get them to recruit you, and then make nice with the guy running everything."

"And if I refuse?" I asked.

Lansky's smile disappeared. He pressed out his smoke with a vengeance and sat upright in his chair. "And why would you wanna do that?" he asked.

"Didn't say I would. I just want to know if the option exists."

Lansky looked at me the way mobsters do sometimes. I was familiar with the look. I'd gotten it from my father on an occasion or three.

Fingers spoke up. "It's part of the job," he said. "And if you want to get out of your little bind..." He let the words fall.

"And what happens to the poor schmuck when I find him?" I asked.

Lansky straightened his tie, then readjusted the bar. I could almost see my reflection. "You really want to know?" he asked.

I guess I didn't. Still, I was left with a choice. Find the guy and let the chips fall where they may or lose my job. But it was more than that. I was being pushed to see just how far I was willing to go. The line in the sand had been drawn by me, not them, and now they wanted to know if I was willing to step over it, and if so, how far I would go.

A lot of people already know I work here," I said.

"Not after today," Fingers countered. "You're fired."

"What?" I said louder than I expected.

"Don't get steamed," Fingers said, then added. "You got pinched, you got fired. That's how the story'll go." He let out a cloud of smoke.

"Don't fret, you're still on the payroll," Lansky added. "But only the three of us will know."

"It needs to look like you got canned and are bitter about it," Fingers added.

I spoke up. "That doesn't sit well," I said. "If you're worried about them hitting this casino, then I need to be here. How am I to do that if I'm fired?" I looked at

Lansky. "Do you think employees might be involved?"

He nodded. "There'd almost have to be in order for the Highwaymen to keep as quiet as they do. There isn't much we know about them. They strike fast and get out quick before anyone's the wiser."

"There's probably a lookout as well," I said. "Better to play the disgruntled employee from the inside than the outside. Fired employees don't hang out in the casino."

I let it sit there. Floating in the cloud of smoke that was gathering above their heads.

Fingers was the first to speak. "He's got a point."

Lansky rubbed his chin and looked down, but not at the table. Who knew what was going through his mind. We waited.

"All right," he said after a moment. "Play it your way. It doesn't matter to me how it gets done, so long as it gets done."

Fingers took a Cuban puff.

"When did they come to town?" I asked.

"Near as we can tell, a couple of weeks ago," Lansky said. "It's not like we can put our finger on an exact date."

"You have any idea how I go about finding these Highwaymen?" I asked.

Lansky shook his head. "None. But you're a bright kid. You'll think of something."

Fingers pulled out an envelope and slid it across the desk. "This is for your expenditures," he said. "You'll probably need to do some gambling."

I looked at the envelope. He was right, of course, but I had seen these types of envelopes slid across tables many times in the past, and I knew what "expenditures" were. I also knew what it meant to accept that envelope— or to not accept it. I picked it up and slid it into the inner pocket of my suit coat.

"Leave a message with Leona if you need me," Fingers said and stood.

Lansky remained seated. He picked up the Luckys and pulled another from the deck. "Don't mess this up, kid," he said.

I stood, shook the hands of both men, then downed my drink for good measure. I nodded at Fingers, then headed for the door.

"Oh, I almost forgot," Lansky said, as he lit the Lucky Strike.

I turned.

"Your father sent me with a message."

"Oh?"

"He said to call your mother."

FOUR

I HATED CHOICES, especially ones that weren't really choices, but what was I to do? I was simply asked to find the guy who was committing a crime. I wasn't responsible for his decisions in life, never mind the consequences of those decisions. Still, I knew what happened when you crossed the mob. There was probably already a hole in the desert with this guy's name on it. Was I to help Lansky fill it?

My week was turning into a dark seven, so I returned to valet, retrieved my car, and headed to my real digs on Seventh Street. "Call your mother" wasn't just a friendly reminder from my father, it was the message he gave me when he needed to talk. Ten minutes later, I pulled into the carport at the side of the house and headed inside. I'd been renting the place from a dame named Kathleen Sithwell, or, more appropriately, from Campbell Realty Company. The small house came fully furnished, which was good because I knew as much about interior design as Liberace knew about pleasing a woman. I'd paid six months up front for the place and was settling in nicely.

I removed the envelope from my suit coat and placed it on the end table. It sat there like an opium pipe in a cigar store, looking up at me. Giving me the same look my priest gave me when I admitted to sipping a bit of the sacrificial wine as a kid. I covered it with the Times, but it didn't help, so I slid open the drawer and stuffed it inside. That would shut it up. I pulled off my lid and tossed it on the couch, then did the same with my suit coat. They made a nice pair. I loosened my tie and picked up the receiver.

"Number please," the female voice said.

"Madison six three five eleven."

"One moment, please."

I waited for a bell on the other end to ring in Boston and my mother to pick up the phone. I knew it would be my mother. It was always my mother. My father never answered the thing, not even once, the whole time I was in the house. My mother would answer it, hold the receiver to her breast, and yell to my father, who would eventually pull himself out of his chair and come to the phone.

"Hello?" my mother said.

"Hi, Ma. It's Max."

"Oh Massimo, it is so good to hear from you. When are you coming home?"

"Not for a while, Ma. I have a job here."

"So this is where you live now?" She asked the question in a way that would have made the Spanish Inquisition cringe.

I ignored it.

"Yes, Ma, this is where I live."

My mother sighed. It was a communal sigh, shared by all Italian mothers, and probably some Jewish ones as well. "So my son's a big shot now and has no time to come see his mother." she pronounced as if she was speaking to someone else, perhaps the operator.

"It's not that, Ma, I'm just working. I'll make time to come see you, don't worry." That would appease her for a short time, probably until Thursday.

"Have you found a good Italian woman to take care of you?" she asked.

This was a setup, and there was no good way to answer it. Say yes and what she would hear is that she is no longer needed. Say no and she would bemoan having to die without grandkids. You see where this is going?

"As soon as I find one as good as the one Dad found, I'll let you know," I said.

Flattery will get you everywhere.

"Oh, Max," she said. I could hear her blushing. "You're as bad as your father."

"Speaking of which," I said, "is he around?"

"He's around here somewhere," she said. She told me she would get him, then yelled out his name so loud I could hear it clearly even through the muffled position of the receiver.

"Who is it?" I heard my father say.

"It's your son, he wants to speak to you." My mother told him, then came back to the phone. "Here's your father," she said to me. "I love you, Massimo, come home."

I told her I loved her but decided not to comment on the second part. What good would it do?

My father took the phone and we both waited for my mother to leave the room, only I couldn't see it happen. It was what she did naturally, well, through years of training anyway. When my father was on the phone, it was best not to be involved in the conversation. My mother had learned that early on and had accepted it, in her own way.

"I heard Lansky came to town," he finally said.

That's my father. All business, no frivolities. There was no "Hi, how ya doing?" Just get to the point and do it quickly. It isn't that he didn't love me—at least I didn't think it was that—it's just that he was a man of few words. He showed his feelings with his actions. In that regard, he was a man of many feelings.

"You heard right," I confirmed.

"He offer you the job?"

"He did."

My father was silent for a moment. It was one of those silences that crawled under your skin and made itself at home. After a moment, he spoke. "He asked me about you."

"You give him a glowing report?" I asked.

"He offered you the job didn't he?"

"That he did," I confirmed.

"And you took it?"

"I guess I did," I said. "It's not like I had a choice, but it doesn't sit well with me."

"You worried about the outcome?"

"I am," I admitted.

"People are responsible for their own actions, Max." It was interesting advice coming from a man whose job it was to make people's mistakes disappear. "People put themselves in a bind. If you want the music, you got to pay the piper. It's not up to you to worry about other people's consequences."

There was my father. He was a good man and he did

what was expected of him, but he wasn't about to stick his neck out for anybody. Not even a stupid kid who took jobs he had no business taking. Still, he knew as well as I did, if Lansky gave you an offer, you accepted it. I worked for mobsters, what did I expect? Candy and roses?

"You need to be careful, Max. These guys aren't people to mess with."

I wasn't sure at first if he was talking about my employers or my quarry. "I know, Dad," I said.

"No, you don't," he countered. "These aren't normal cheats. They rely completely on anonymity to function the way they do. They hit hard and leave before anyone is the wiser, always on the circuit. And there's usually an inside man."

"Yeah," I said. "Lansky told me that part."

"Did he tell you they're not above murder?"

"Funny," I said, "he left that part out."

"Play this smart, Max," my father cautioned. "Call me if you need me." And with that, he hung up.

After the phone call ended, I went back to the end table and opened the drawer. The envelope was still inside, as were its contents, still looking at me the same way. I pulled it out and let it sit heavily in my hand for a few minutes, then I went into the kitchen, got a screwdriver and a chair and returned to the living room. The chair helped me reach the vent and the screwdriver helped me get the cover off. I placed the envelope inside, up high, where no one would look, and returned the cover to its original position.

FIVE

I HAD A late date that evening, one that would keep me up a while, so I decided a bit of shut-eye was in order. I wasn't much of a napper, but it had been a full day so far. I'd committed a crime, been sent to the big house, and was tasked with preparing a guy for his mansion in the desert. If that didn't require a nap, a shower, and a shave, I don't know what did.

I tried to lie down, but it didn't take. All I could think of was how I was supposed to find a group of people who specialized in not being found. Fingers and Lansky were expecting me to go undercover. To play the part of the disgruntled employee. That was all well and good, if I only knew where to begin. But I didn't have a clue. It was times like these that I wished I smoked. Since it was clear a little shut-eye wasn't in my future, I got up and decided to hit the showers.

By the time I wiped the Barbasol from my face, I was in a much better mood. It's amazing what smooth skin will do for a man's disposition, makes him eager for the glad rags. I chose a plum, two-button, three-patch pocket corduroy coat and gray slacks. I knotted a navy blue tie around my neck and stuffed a matching square in the top pocket of my suit coat. I shot my cuffs, then slipped a plum feather in the bowtie band of my lid before positioning it into place on my noggin. I ran my forefinger and thumb around the brim, just for good measure. I believe the proper word was dapper.

It was turning into a beautiful desert night, so I left the top down on my bright red Roadmaster, climbed in, and after starting the beast, headed to Twelfth and Clark to pick up my date for the evening, Virginia James.

"Just a moment," she said after letting me in. "I'm not quite ready, but I will be in two shakes of a lamb's tail."

Virginia's apartment looked as if it came off the pages of *Ladies' Home Journal* or *Good Housekeeping*, possibly even *Cosmo*. The furnishings, as well as the apartment itself, were courtesy of the Sands Hotel and Casino, or more specifically Jack Entratter—the manager of the Copa Room at the Sands, and Virginia's boss. Virginia was a Copa Girl and a leggy one at that. She had long brown hair, matching eyes, and broad Texas shoulders. A whiff of lavender filled the air as she walked by.

I had been seeing Virginia since the untimely departure of her previous roommate, Jeanie Gardner, who had recently been assigned a new bunkie at the state pen. I wouldn't say Virginia was my girl, but I might sock you one in the eye if you tried to take her.

When Virginia emerged from the bathroom, she was wearing a bright blue swing dress with white polka dots, a white collar, and a wide black belt that wrapped around her waist like a teenage boy. This night Virginia had her hair done pageboy style, the bottoms curling nicely around her ears on each side. Her lips were red and her eyes dark, but, honestly, I didn't get much past the lips.

"Is your top up or down?" she asked.

"Down," I said. "Like any good top should be."

"You're impertinent," she said as she opened a drawer and pulled out a scarf. She tied it around her head, slipped on matching gloves, and picked up her pocketbook. Then she walked over and kissed me softly on the cheek.

I might have blushed.

"You, my dear, are a vision," I said.

That got me a warm smile.

We piled into the Roadmaster and headed for what was quickly becoming a favorite locals' haunt, the Bootlegger. They had late performances, which was perfect, because Virginia did two shows on a Friday night, and that would allow us to still make an evening of it. We were there to take in a jazz group called The Five and Dimes. We were also to meet Nancy Williams. Nancy, like Virginia, was a dancer, but she wasn't a Copa Girl. Instead, she was a Dice Girl, part of a troop that performed nightly at the El Rancho. Virginia and Nancy had formed a kinship and Nancy was dating one of the musicians, Jimmy Five of the Five and Dimes. This was to be my first meeting for both the band and the dancer.

Nancy was already seated when we arrived, having reserved a table toward the front. Like Virginia, Nancy wore a swing dress, only hers was powder pink with black polka dots and a matching sash around the middle. She stood to greet us and the two women hugged.

"This is Max," Virginia said. "He's the one I told you about." She turned and sent me a wink.

I extended my hand. "How do you do?" I said.

Nancy took it and squeezed lightly. "You were right," she said to Virginia. "He is a handsome one."

Who was I to argue?

A waitress came to take our order. I went for a manhattan, while the ladies both ordered a tom collins. It seemed to be a dancer's drink. We took our seats. Virginia sat next to Nancy and I next to my date.

"Tell me about yourself," Nancy said. She pulled a slim cigarette from a pack, put one to her pink lips, and offered another to Virginia.

"What's there to tell?" I asked, picking the lighter up from the table. "I came here for a bachelor party and fell in love with the place."

"Your party?" she asked.

I lit the two cigarettes with a grin. "Kid brother of a friend," I said.

Virginia placed a soft hand on Nancy's arm and shook her head slightly. She didn't want me to see it, but I did anyway.

Nancy was as leggy as my Virginia, but not as broad in the shoulders and not nearly as tall. Even in her heels, she was lucky if she stood five-six. She had light brown hair, a full smile, and innocent eyes. I wondered how long it would take Vegas to change that.

"Your turn," I said. "From whence do you hail?"

"I'm a California girl. Born and raised," she admitted proudly. "Came here to dance in forty-eight. I was offered a two-week contract at the El Rancho, and I've been there ever since."

"Been longer than two weeks," I said.

She smiled brightly. "That it has."

The waitress came with our drinks. I slipped her a Lincoln and asked her to fill our glasses again when they went dry.

"Nancy owns a dance studio now," Virginia offered.

"Isn't that nice," I said and took a sip. "Curtain climbers?" I asked.

Nancy chuckled. "Not quite that small," she said. "But young none-the-less."

"That must keep you busy," I said.

"It does. I teach during the day, after rehearsals of course, dance at night, and in my free time I sew costumes for our recitals."

I began to lament my wasted life, so before I found a tower to fling myself off of, I let the dancers talk while I gave the place the once over, just to see what I could see. The small room, though filled to capacity, was inviting. Fancy chandeliers, looking more like they belonged in a ballroom than a jazz club, dangled from the ceiling. The walls were covered with smartly patterned paper. Thick, heavy curtains framed the small stage, but the nine-piece band seemed to make it work. There were trombones, trumpets, and two saxophones—a bari and a tenor—though I wondered what happened to the alto. A lad in a pork pie hat but no coat sat, sleeves rolled up, behind a trap set with a hi-hat and three crash cymbals. Another like-minded fellow took his position behind an electric keyboard. A young man with a loose tie and no hat took the upright bass.

Jimmy Five stepped on stage, and the band immediately went into action. The drummer hit the distinctive swing beat, followed by the keyboardist. The bari sax player apparently had an alto hiding in his pocket, because while his bari rested in the stand, he placed the much smaller alto to his mouth and joined in. The tone was soft, easy, and effortless. I recognized it right away, *Take Five*. Jimmy jumped in and began to croon.

"Won't you stop and take a little time out with me," he began, playing up to the crowd. "Just take five. Stop your busy day and take the time out to see if I'm alive."

He had a smooth voice that fit nicely with the music. The crowd agreed and showed him so with tapping feet and nodding heads.

When the tune was finished, after a respectable pause for clapping, they went right into *Doodlin'*, *New Rhumba*, and *'Round Midnight*. Jimmy was engaging. He sang, spoke to the crowd, and even, at times, to the band. There was laughter and applause, and just general merriment. The crowd was enjoying the band and the band was enjoying the music. What more could you ask for?

After the sixth song, *On the Sunny Side of the Street*, the band took a break as Jimmy announced each musician, giving them a solo in turn as the keyboardist, drummer, and bass player kept time. When he got to the keyboardist, the band went quiet except for the drummer and bassist.

"Ladies and gentlemen, we're incredibly lucky to have a special guest with us tonight. All the way from New Orleans, Louisiana..."

"New Orleans, Louisiana," the band repeated behind him.

The crowd laughed.

Jimmy turned to face the band as they seemed to share a private joke. He turned back to the crowd and continued. "By way of Los Angeles, California." He paused and waited for the band to repeat the city's name.

They didn't, which only caused the crowd to laugh harder.

But before he could get his next words out, the band yelled, "Los Angeles, California."

The crowd roared.

Jimmy, who was laughing as well, continued. "Making

a guest appearance here tonight." He looked toward the keyboardist. "And possibly for a while longer."

The man shrugged.

"Vinny 'Keys' Collins on the electric ivories!" Jimmy yelled.

The crowd cheered. Apparently, Vinny "Keys" Collins was known to them. I had never heard of the man.

Keys played a lengthy solo, greatly encouraged by the crowd and the band.

He was good. Very good.

When the solo concluded, the band went immediately into their next tune. A nice arrangement featuring the trumpets, called Jordu. Jimmy didn't sing but kept time by swinging his hand and arm, playing the part of conductor. It wasn't needed, but I guess it gave him something to do. I got into the piece when the tenor sax joined in.

By the time the band took a short break, we were well into our second round.

"Jimmy should come over and say hi," Nancy said.

"That'll be nice," Virginia added.

Nancy was right. Jimmy did come to our table, but he wasn't alone.

SIX

WHEN HE CAME to the table, Jimmy Five was in the company of the man he introduced on keyboard, Vinny "Keys" Collins. The two men were in direct contrast. Jimmy, being the front man, was as shiny as a copper penny. He wore a gold, broadcloth jacket, with narrow lapels and patterned with a heavy chain motif. His shirt was white and his thin tie black, as was the square in his pocket and his slacks. His shoes were gold wingtips and his hair wound up in a high pompadour.

His companion, on the other hand, was as casual as could be. The sleeves of his white shirt were rolled up past the elbows and his single-knotted maroon tie hung loose around his neck. He kept his top button open, and his pork pie hat sat askew on his head, topping his disheveled hair. He had one of those faces that, despite his age, seemed to have stories to tell. A cigarette dangled precariously from his mouth.

We stood as they approached.

Jimmy leaned in and kissed Nancy on the cheek. "These are my friends," she said. "Virginia and Max."

We all shook hands.

"This is Keys," Jimmy said.

Keys tipped his hat. I guess mobsters aren't the only ones with clever nicknames.

"I didn't think you'd mind if he tags along," Jimmy added.

"Certainly not," Virginia said, a little too enthusiastically for my taste.

After another round of handshakes, Keys pulled a chair over and we all squeezed around the table. The waitress approached. "Can I get you gentlemen a drink?" she asked.

Jimmy ordered a sloe gin fizz, while Keys ordered rye, straight up.

I was skeptical. You can never trust a man who drinks rye. I should know. I drink it.

I tapped the waitress' arm. "Put it on my tab," I said.

Jimmy thanked me. Keys just nodded. He reached across the table and took Nancy's lighter. "Mind if I use this?" he asked, without waiting for an answer. I thought I detected a bit of a Cajun accent. He lit his smoke and took in a deep breath, as if he'd been on a faraway island where cigarettes were as foreign as modesty in Vegas. He held the smoke in for a time before leaning back in his chair, tilting his head, and gleefully blowing it out his nose. "Awwww," he said, letting the expression trail off.

Virginia laughed.

I did not.

Keys hooked an arm around the back of his chair and set his right ankle on his left knee. "So what's the tale with you cats?" he asked, before taking another puff.

Cats? I thought.

Jimmy spoke up. "Nancy and Virginia are dancers. Virginia's a Copa Girl at the Sands and my Nancy's a Dice Girl at the El Rancho." Jimmy looked to me. "I'm sorry, but I don't know what you do."

"He works at the Sands," Virginia said. "Though I couldn't tell you what he does either."

I had told Virginia of my employment but opted not to go into detail. I wasn't quite sure where the job would take me, and I was even less sure where the two of us were headed, so it seemed best to be vague.

"Special projects," I offered. "A little of this, a little of that."

Virginia twisted her mouth and shook her head, "That's what he always says. But it doesn't mean anything."

"The Sands, huh?" Keys asked. "How long you been there?"

"Not long," I said. "Just enough to get to know the place."

Keys laughed. I wondered what was funny.

"Nice group you got," I said to Jimmy. "Great sound."

"Thanks," Jimmy said. "We're a little short tonight, but we're making it work."

"Short?" I asked.

"There's supposed to be ten in the band, eleven with me. You know, five and dimes. We're short two, though. Thankfully, Keys here is filling up one spot."

"Who else is missing?" Virginia asked.

"The alto," I said.

Jimmy looked at me curiously. "You got a good eye," he said. "How'd you know it was the alto?"

"All the other spots were filled. Your sax man is good

35

on the alto, but he's much better on the bari."

"You play?" Keys asked.

"Used to," I said.

"Why don't you join us?" he offered.

I'm not sure who at the table was most surprised by the offer: me, the girls, or Jimmy.

"Oh no," I said, putting up my hands in protest.

"I didn't know you play the saxophone," Virginia said.

"Played," I emphasized. "Something I haven't done for years. Haven't even picked up the thing. I don't even know if I could make a sound come out."

"Just like riding a bike," Keys said. "Once the music is in your blood, man, it stays there."

"He doesn't have a sax," Jimmy said.

"I'm sure Johnny Boy will let him use his," Keys countered.

"Or a reed," I added.

"C'mon, man. You know how sax players are," Keys said. "They've always got ten or fifteen reeds on them. They split so easily."

All eyes were on me as I looked from face to face around the table.

"Better make up your mind soon," Jimmy said as he stood. "We're on in ten."

And here I thought the man was on my side.

"C'mon, man. Let's hear what you got," Keys said.

"What I got," I assured him, "is likely not worth hearing."

"Only one way to find out," Keys said. He sat up, crushed his smoke out in the ashtray, and stood.

I looked to Virginia. She had an excited smile. It was obvious what she wanted me to do, and I'd be lying if I said I didn't feel a bit of a nostalgic tinge at the thought myself. I'd played the instrument for several years and had once been considered quite talented with the thing—even considered going professional. But that was a lifetime ago.

"All right," I said. I downed what was left of my manhattan and stood. "I'll give it a go."

The two men took me backstage and introduced me to the band. Johnny Boy was none-too-happy to relinquish his sax, but after a little encouragement from Keys, he relented, even handing me a new reed. I put the thing in my mouth to get it wet and softened. A vibrating reed is what makes the sound on a saxophone, and for that to happen, the reed needs a little softening up so it won't split. Even after all these years, the taste of the cane was familiar.

Johnny Boy removed the used reed and washed the mouthpiece off by dipping it in his glass of scotch. I guess if that didn't kill the germs, nothing would. I rested the reed he gave me against the mouthpiece and tightened it in place with the ligature. I stuffed the thing in my mouth, hoping the correct embouchure would come back to me. I curled my bottom lip over my lower row of teeth, tightened my jaw, and blew into the mouthpiece as a test. It squeaked loudly.

Johnny Boy shook his head.

Keys laughed. "You'll get it, man. Don't worry."

I'd bitten too tightly on the reed. I slid the mouthpiece onto the cork at the neck of the sax, up to the indentation that was already there. I threw the neck strap over my head, hooked it to the body of the sax, and prepared to try again. This time I didn't bite down so hard.

A note came out. It was a C-sharp. Not a good C-sharp, but a C-sharp none-the-less. Enough to gain a raised eyebrow from Johnny. It was also enough to give me a shot of courage. I wiggled my fingers on the keys, playing with the action, then took the mouthpiece between my teeth and blew again. This time I remembered to open my throat. I shot up a scale and then back down. The keys felt comfortable and my fingers seemed to still know just where to go. I played a couple more scales, just to warm up—my tone smoother than I expected.

Johnny Boy stepped over to me, bari in hand. He placed the instrument in his mouth and blew a consistent A, holding it steady.

I blew an A as well, then adjusted the mouthpiece until the waves in the sound disappeared.

He followed it with an F-sharp, which I matched until my instrument was tuned.

"Nice tone," he said. "We'll play off the same sheet. You take the top line."

I nodded and followed him on stage. I was glad I had my coat on to hide the stains that were surely under each armpit.

"When Jimmy comes on stage," Johnny Boy said. "We hit *Take the 'A' Train*."

"Got it," I said, hoping my bravado was enough to stop my teeth from chattering.

Jimmy stepped on stage, and the band began. To my surprise, I held my own and by the time we'd hit the third song, *Freddie Freeloader*, I was beginning to really feel the beat. It's not that I didn't make mistakes—I certainly made enough of those, but my fingers seemed to not only remember the notes, but were eager to get to them. And Johnny Boy helped guide me along the way. My speed increased and my tone smoothed out. By the fifth song, I was hitting on all eights.

Keys was right. Once the music is in you, it never leaves.

At the end of the set, Jimmy made a special point of saying I was sitting in with the group. I even performed half a solo, much to the crowd's delight. I looked over at Virginia. Her eyes were sparkling. When it was all over, I handed the alto back to Johnny Boy and thanked him.

"How much do I owe you for the reed?" I asked.

"Keep it," he said. "And go pick yourself up a sax. You should be playing."

I thanked him, and we shook hands.

Jimmy came over. "That was great, man! You're sure swingin' with that thing. You ought to sit in more often."

I thanked him and told him I would consider it.

"You got good chops," he said. "Don't waste 'em."

Keys came next, wearing a smile. He slapped his hand into mine. "Very impressive," he said. "I knew you had it in you. Want to step outside for a smoke?"

"Sure," I said and followed him to the back door. I was floating on a bit of a cloud. Like I'd downed four manhattans. The desert's a different place at night. When the sun goes down, it pulls all the heat with it, leaving a strange silence in its wake. There was a slight breeze and the cool night air felt good on my neck.

Keys removed his lid and pulled something from the inside band. He replaced the lid, slipped the item into his mouth, then set fire to the tip. It wasn't a cigarette. He inhaled deeply and held it in, then pulled it from his lips and offered it to me.

I shook my head.

After a moment, he let out his breath. "Aren't ya stickin'?" he asked.

"Not my cup of chowder," I said.

"You don't know what you're missing," he countered, as he put the thing back to his lips and inhaled twice more. "Blasting the weed tends to put things into perspective," he said as he blew out the puff.

I wasn't sure how much perspective I could handle.

One of the trumpeters came out the door. "You layin' down the hustle?" he asked Keys.

Keys nodded.

"Gimme an ace," he said, then paused. "Better make it a deck."

Keys reached into his pocket and pulled out a small bag. He handed it to the man and received a five spot for his trouble. The trumpeter went back inside.

"You were pretty good with that thing," Keys said, motioning to the door.

I told him I appreciated it and admitted that it felt nice to pick the sax up again. It had been too many years.

"What got you into playing?" Keys asked.

"A girl," I admitted.

Keys let out a hearty laugh and slapped his leg. "Oh," he said. "You gotta tell me about this."

"I picked up the instrument in sixth grade," I began. "My parents took me to the high school band's open house. I'm not sure what they were thinking, but they had been encouraging me to pick up an instrument for some time. I wanted to learn the piano, but my father refused to buy one. He told me I wouldn't practice it anyway."

"Yeah, yeah. Get to the girl," Keys said.

"Anyway, I was walking around the room, when I saw this dish in a tight sweater sitting in a chair and playing the alto saxophone. She was the spitting image of Marlene Dietrich, and I was in love. She could have been playing the kazoo and I would've picked it up. My parents couldn't drag me away from her. I even ended up taking lessons from her, though not for long."

"Why's that?" Keys asked.

"My father was right; I didn't take to practicing. In fact, I hated it, but I loved playing."

"That's the best way to practice anyway," Keys said.

"Probably," I admitted.

I sat there for a bit while memories of the sax girl in her sweater filled my head. Keys must have known because he let me have my moment. I had loved her more than the instrument when I started, but eventually it was the other way around. It was fine; I was saving myself for Joi Lansing anyway.

"I guess we'd better get back inside," I said. "The girls will be wondering what happened to me."

"What're you doing tomorrow?" Keys asked.

"I'm not sure yet, why?"

He pulled out what looked like a business card and wrote something on the back. "Here's my room number. I'm staying at the El Rancho," he said. "Give me a call and we'll go pick you up a sax."

I took the card.

"Now before you say no," he said, "just think it over. Music's in your blood. I can tell."

He was probably right.

By the time we got back to the table, Jimmy was already seated with the girls.

"Jimmy was just telling us what a great job you did," Virginia said.

"He's just being kind," I offered.

"No, man. That ain't my bit when it comes to music," Jimmy said. "No apple butter here, just honest to goodness respect."

Virginia was beaming. When I sat down, she pulled next to me and wrapped herself around my arm. I didn't mind.

"I meant what I said before," Jimmy continued. "We're short a sax. You're welcome to fill in."

"We're going to get one tomorrow," Keys offered.

I cautioned. "Now don't go getting ahead of yourself. I haven't agreed to anything."

Keys looked to Jimmy. The two men shared a knowing smile, an inside joke perhaps. "You will," Keys said. "Once the music is in your blood..."

"I know," I said, cutting him off. "It stays there."

"Right as rain," Keys said.

There was one more set before the night was through, but I wasn't part of it. After the band finished, we said our goodbyes. Keys reminded me to call him tomorrow, then Virginia and I headed to the Roadmaster. I opened the door for my date, but instead of getting in, she turned, pulled me by the lapels, and kissed me fully on the lips. My knees almost buckled. What could I do? I kissed her right back and for several minutes we took turns exchanging pleasantries. Something in her kisses told me she wasn't just interested in a game of backseat bingo.

She slipped into the passenger seat, with the grace only a dancer could achieve. I tossed my lid into the back seat, headed to my side of the car, then pointed the beast in the direction of Virginia's apartment—her hand on my leg the entire time. I might have driven a bit faster than the posted speed.

When we got to her place, I jumped out and opened her side of the door. Her legs came out first. They were a fine set—long and slender, though muscular in all the right places. As she stood, her dress fell into place. Then she kissed me again for good measure.

"You're a man of many mysteries," she said. "What other secrets are in there?"

"If I tell you, they won't be secrets."

She placed her palms on my chest. "So you play the saxophone."

"I suppose I do."

She concentrated on my chest for a moment, rubbing her hands up and down my jacket. Then she looked up at me with a familiar sparkle in her eye. "My musician," she said. "Would you like to come in and see my etchings?"

"Isn't that supposed to be my line?" I asked.

"Would you like to come in and show me your etchings?"

"Man would I!"

As Virginia slid the key in and unlocked her apartment, I vowed to buy a saxophone the very next day.

SEVEN

THE NEXT MORNING I woke up alone. I had expected it though, Virginia had an early morning practice; they were learning a new routine. I'd thought she might wake me, but instead, she decided to let me sleep. That's my girl. It was Saturday and I had only one thing on the agenda. I took the card Keys had given me from the pocket of my slacks. It had his name—Vinny "Keys" Collins—on one side and underneath it said "Musician, Boozehound, Grifter."

I picked up Virginia's phone and asked the operator to connect me to the El Rancho. When PBX answered, I asked for the room Keys had written down. It rang several times, without an answer, so I decided to head to my place to gussy up a bit. Virginia and I were getting cozy, but not to the stage where toiletries were involved.

As I was closing up the apartment, the superintendent showed. He was a dark-haired man, one who needed to step a bit closer to the razor when he shaved. He wore dark blue trousers and a sweat-stained t-shirt with the sleeves rolled up. A pack of smokes was wrapped in the sleeve over his left shoulder. Steak and potatoes didn't stand a ghost of a chance in this man's house.

"Long night?" he asked.

"Just checking in," I said.

He raised an eyebrow, wrinkling his forehead, and accompanied it with a mouth twisted to one side. "Virginia's not here," he assured me.

"And neither am I," I countered.

"You been spendin' a lot of time here lately."

I turned to face the man. I wasn't sure what business it was of his. "Is that going to be a problem?" I asked.

"Not with me," he said. "I'm only the supe."

He might have meant "snoop," I couldn't tell.

The man turned to leave, so I headed home. When I got in the front door, the phone was ringing. I didn't usually get too many calls, so I decided I should probably answer the thing.

It was Leona.

"Hold for Mr. Abbandandolo," she said.

I held.

"You comin' in today, Max?" He asked when he came on the line.

"Hadn't planned on it," I said. "It is Saturday after all."

"You better come in," he said. "That Elizabeth lady is yapping her trap, asking for you. I don't know how much more anyone can take."

Lizzie. I had completely forgotten about her. "I gotta shower and shave," I said.

"Late start?" he asked.

"Late night," I assured him.

"Good for you," Fingers said. "Now get in here."

I hung up the phone and looked at the vent. I thought I could hear laughing.

I took a quick shower—getting significantly friendlier with the razor than had my blue-collar friend. I chose a more conservative suit than what I had on the night before. Navy blue with a maroon patterned tie and matching square. Somehow plum didn't seem an appropriate color for a house dick. I put on my shoulder holster and slipped my .38 into place. Fingers had never told me to wear the thing at work, but then again, he'd never told me not to.

I had been given a parking spot at the front of the casino, so this time I put the Roadmaster where it belonged and went inside. I probably should've gone to the tables, but something made me head upstairs instead. I walked over to a nondescript door in a nondescript hallway, easily missed if one wasn't looking. That was intentional. I gave a light rap and waited. A small door slid open and a set of eyes peeked through. It was the same system used in speakeasies during prohibition. The small door slid back closed and the big door opened.

I stepped from the mezzanine into a whole different world. I was up inside the ceiling. A place filled with pipes, tubes, and wires—the parts of a building hidden from its occupants. Among the support beams was a set of catwalks that traveled above the table games. They were used by surveillance to watch the players below. To make sure no one was tempted to cheat. Mobsters really did invent Las Vegas.

The casino ceiling was constructed of one-way mirrored glass. If you looked up, all you saw was a reflection of yourself and the table you were playing on, along with all the tables and players in the entire pit—depending on how far you wanted to look. Few people, however, looked up. This was something my father had taught me as a young lad. "If you want to hide something," he'd say. "If you have to leave something to be picked up later, something you can't take with you right away, always hide it above eye level. People don't look up." I found that to be true.

Except, of course, for pit bosses. They used the mirrored ceiling to keep track of more than one table at a time. Glancing upward, nonchalantly, hundreds of times a day.

Above the glass were men walking the catwalk, keeping an eye on all the players, especially anyone identified by the pit boss. Looking down through the ceiling was like looking into a window, only the people looking up couldn't see you. If a pit boss was worried about something or someone, he need only call surveillance and the matter would be looked into. It was fair to say that most gamblers had no idea there was an entire system of employees, directly above them, keeping a close eye on the goings on.

Charlie was one of those employees. He was a short man, who walked with a bit of a limp. He wore glasses that had been made from the bottom of pop bottles. A strap ran across the back of his head to keep the glasses from falling off his face when he leaned over the railing to have a better look.

"Hello, Mr. Rossi," he said.

"Hey, Charlie. The whale still at the table?"

"Yeah, you want to see him?"

"I do."

Charlie turned and headed down the catwalk. I followed. It was like walking the gangway of a ship, only more stable. We made our way to the center where all the catwalks connected, then took another to the right, heading to the portion of the pit that housed the poker tables. Our whale was below. He was sitting in the fifth spot and had a stack of chips to his right and a drink to his left. Lizzie was also to his left. She had on a red circle dress, with matching flats, gloves, and purse. She was tapping her fingers on the table, but it wasn't to music. Besides the whale, there were two other players, a dealer, and the pit boss, who was standing close—but not too close—to one side.

"How long has he been here?" I asked.

"Couple of hours," Charlie said.

"How long did he stay last night?"

"I don't know," Charlie said. "I was told he disappeared for a while."

"Probably went back to his suite to rest," I said.

I looked down at the man. He was big. Built like a bull or a prizefighter. I could see it even under his suit coat. He had all the trappings of wealth—Stetson hat, complete with bowtie ribbon; fitted suit, single-breasted, with a matching vest; white shirt; patternless tie and matching square—yet, somehow, it all looked wrong on him. I couldn't see his feet, but I was willing to bet his shoes were wingtip and his socks coordinated. It was as if Cary Grant had dressed him for a movie role.

I watched the big man's hands. They were thick, yet nimble. His left rested on the table while the right repeatedly broke a short stack of chips in two, then shuffled them again into one. The activity was performed without the whale even looking at his hand, as if it were on autopilot. He was chinning, but it wasn't possible to hear what he was saying.

As the game continued, the big man looked everywhere but his cards. Even at one point staring straight up as if he could see me. I instinctively took a step backward.

"A little disturbing, isn't it?" Charlie said. "The first time it happened to me I 'bout fell over the rail backward,

I jumped so fast. But don't worry, they can't see us."

It was little solace.

"What'd he buy in for?" I asked.

"Two large,"

I let out a long whistle.

"You can say that again," Charlie added. "And he's built upon that already."

"Cheating?" I asked.

Charlie shook his head. "Not that I can tell. This guy seems to know his Bees. See what he's doing with those chips?" he said pointing over the railing. "That's a man who's used to sitting at the table, but not the side he's on."

"Dealer?" I asked.

Charlie nodded. "Most likely."

Not that it was illegal to gamble in another casino if you were a dealer, but it was frowned upon and not something dealers typically did. After spending eight hours with cards in your hand, the last thing most dealers wanted to do was gamble somewhere else. Of course, there were always exceptions to the rule. Some people enjoyed a busman's holiday.

"Anything unusual?" I asked.

Charlie hesitated. He looked away for a moment, then back at me. "Not really," he finally said.

"Spill it," I said.

"It's nothing. It's just that I can't help but feel I've seen him somewhere before."

"Here in the casino?"

Charlie twisted his face. "No, not here. I would have remembered that."

"Then where?"

"That's just it. I have a good memory for faces,"

Charlie said. "But I can't seem to put my finger on this one."

I hadn't known Charlie long, but in that time I found he was right. He did have a good memory for faces. In fact, that's why they hired him. Once he saw you, he typically never forgot you. The Sands relied on that. But Charlie was like a bloodhound on a scent. Once he got something in his head, he'd keep going until he figured it out. He wouldn't let it rest; it was just a matter of time before it came to him. I needed to get down there, so I bid Charlie farewell, and told him to let me know when his memory kicked in.

EIGHT

YOU NEVER REALLY know a man until you play cards with him. How he bluffs, his tells, when he'll take a chance, and when he won't. Does he have the guts to stay in and see it through, or the smarts to cut his losses when he's too far behind? I needed to know a bit more about Mr. Richard Dorsey, our high roller, so I decided a game of poker was in order.

It's not like the Sands only had one high roller, it's just that some whales seemed to command more attention than others. This was one of those whales. Besides, he was winning and in poker that meant the house was winning too. High rollers playing poker bring in large pots and with the house making ten percent off every one of them—win or lose—Fingers and his boys were making a nice bit of lettuce off of this goose. They'd do everything they could to keep him planted in his seat without distraction.

Dorsey was still sitting in the fifth spot when I arrived

at the table. I hadn't expected him to move. Lizzie, on the other hand, was MIA. The two other players were in the second and third spots. I took the first spot. It wasn't my favorite place to be, but it allowed me to get a good look at things. I laid my lid and a C-note on the table and waited to be dealt in.

"Looks like we have a new victim," the whale said in a booming baritone. "You'll have to wait until I beat these two," he added.

The table was playing draw poker, which meant our whale was either a poker purist, or he didn't take to the more complicated versions of the game, such as Texas hold 'em. Draw poker was simple in concept. Each player is given five cards, face down. Bets are made off that initial deal. Afterward, each player is allowed to discard up to three cards and have them replaced with new ones from the dealer. Another round of betting takes place and then there's the final stage, called the showdown, where everyone left in the game shows their hands. Highest hand takes the pot—minus the house's cut, of course.

They were in the final stage of betting.

The man next to me was dressed in a blue cardigan sweater, white slacks, and a white shirt with no tie or lid. It was the weekend, after all. He had hesitation written all over him. He fiddled with his chips with one hand and rubbed his chin raw with the other. I couldn't identify all the chips in the pot, but it looked substantial. Clearly, he felt he had a good hand, but lacked the courage to pull the pin. His doubt had overtaken him.

When a gambler doesn't pay attention to the cards and the other players, he is left to make all his decisions on what could be, not what was. If you can't see the signs in front of you, you have no business playing with the big dogs.

The whale was still fiddling with his chips. I got a better look at him from this angle. He was a big man with thick eyebrows, a broad nose, and a tight jaw you could probably see through in the right light. "You gonna put your big boy pants on and bet?" he asked, as he took a drink. "Or should we order in?"

The cardigan's eyes narrowed. After another moment he folded.

The dealer collected his cards.

"Atta boy," The whale said.

The man next to him had on a military-style shirt and matching pants with creases stronger than black coffee. He wore a simple tie and a tight brown leather belt that was probably ironed as well. He threw in his chips.

"No more bets," the dealer said, waving his hand over the pot like Houdini. It was a signal to Charlie and the boys that the betting had ceased.

"Let's see what you got," the whale said to the military man.

He laid down a pair of kings with a smile, then put a pair of queens on top of it. His other card was a nine. Two pair.

"Nice hand," the whale said as he laid a five of clubs on the table, followed by a six and seven of spades. "I probably would have bet big too." He paused and laid down an eight of diamonds. "Too bad it came when I had a gutshot that turned into a straight." His final card came next. It was a nine. The suit didn't matter at this point. He had a straight and a straight beats two pair any day.

But it made me wonder what would make a man draw to an inside straight. It was called a gutshot for a reason. Anyone who plays the Bees knows it's a fool's hand. The odds of getting the card you need are slim to none. It's a lure, a shiny object dangled in the face of the inexperienced—or people with nothing to lose.

The military man wasn't happy, but the cardigan was even less so. "Bollocks!" he exclaimed. "I had a flush."

The whale laughed hard. "Well, if that's true, then you need a bigger pair of brass clankers."

I was surprised when the cardigan didn't get up and leave.

"Can I get this filled?" the whale said, holding up his drink glass.

The pit boss motioned to a cocktail waitress. "Get Mr. Dorsey another whiskey."

"Where's my dealer?" Dorsey said to the pit boss. "This one doesn't feel lucky to me. I don't like the cut of his jib."

The pit boss stepped closer to the table. He was a sturdy man, with sturdy shoulders. His hair was parted to the side and he sported a Gable mustache. A solid tie capped off his pin-striped suit and matching vest. "Hollis is on break, Mr. Dorsey. But I can get you a different dealer until he returns."

"How about we just wait?"

"As you wish."

It was amazing what high rollers could get away with. Anything to keep them on the tables. Want a drink? We got you. Want to eat your meal at the table? We'll get you an extra napkin. Want a specific dealer? You got it. Just stay at the tables and lay your lettuce down.

We waited until Hollis was done with his break. Luckily, he only had a few minutes left, as he turned up out of nowhere and took over the dealing duties. I knew it was him from the nametag above his chest. He changed my biscuit into twenty individual chips, sliding the bill into a metal box at the side of the table, and began shuffling the single deck of cards. Watching a dealer shuffle is a thing of beauty. They split the deck in two, then mix the cards in rapid succession, over and over, all without creating even the slightest bend or crease. If you think it's easy, you ought to try it.

When Hollis was almost finished shuffling, he got a curious look on his face. "Excuse me," he said, then quickly turned to the side and sneezed violently into a handkerchief he yanked from his pocket.

The pit boss turned.

"Whoa there," the whale said. "That's quite a sneeze."

Hollis wiped his nose, replaced the handkerchief, and turned back to the table, all under the watchful eye of the pit boss. "I'm sorry for the interruption," he said. He finished shuffling, pushed the cards in front of the whale, and asked him to cut the deck.

The whale did as asked with his left hand, then returned that hand to its original spot on the table. It struck me as curious as I'd expected him to use his right. After all, it was the hand with which he so nimbly sorted the chips.

While most dealers stand while dealing, poker dealers sit at the center of the table, which itself is lower than tables for other games like craps, blackjack, or even roulette. I wasn't entirely sure why. Perhaps it was a throwback from the old saloon days, or perhaps it was because poker takes longer to play than other games. A ball doesn't take much time to bounce around a spinning wheel and fall into place; blackjack ends as soon as anyone reaches or goes over twenty-one; and craps... well, craps is just confusing. Poker, on the other hand, is more like chess—a game of strategy. A thinking man's game.

Poker tends to be a game of quiet examination, not boisterous projection. Of course, some people do bluff by trying to annoy their opponents, but those types of players rarely last. Most poker players, the good ones anyway, watch their opponents more than they do the cards. They look for signs—"tells" they're called—that key you in to what the person is thinking. Putting a hand too quickly on your chips means you're eager to bet, which tells those paying attention you've got a good hand. Some people play with their faces, trying to look nonchalant when the cards favor them. Others get nervous, tapping things, or repeatedly look at their cards.

Cards don't change. You don't need to keep looking at them.

The cocktail waitress returned with a drink. The whale casually tossed a chip on her tray with his right hand. At the same time, he moved his left to his lap. The waitress asked if I wanted anything, but this was business, not pleasure, so I passed, and returned my attention to the whale.

The whale looked up at me with surprise. "What are you lookin' at?" he asked.

"Just watching the game," I said. "It's how you play."

His eyes narrowed. "Yeah? Well, it looks to me like you're watching more than the game," he said. "Maybe you should mind your own beeswax."

"Perhaps, I should."

I was the player to the left of the dealer, so it was my job to throw in the ante, which is just the amount you have to put down even to get cards. I tossed in one chip. The cardigan threw in his chip and one more just for fun. This was called the straddle. It wasn't something seen very often, except by serious players. The cardigan was trying to gain back his dignity. I doubt it would work.

The military man threw his two chips into the pot, as did the whale. When it came back to me, I added in my missing chip. That triggered Hollis. He slid one card, face down, in front of each player, one at a time, until we all had five cards.

The whale peeked at his cards with his left hand. He glanced casually at the cardigan and then the military man before returning to his drink.

I looked at my five. It wasn't anything to write home about. A couple of threes, a two, a seven, and one lonely jack. Two hearts, two spades, and a club. It was just about as bad a hand as you could get, so I threw five chips into the pot. That got the whale's attention.

"Ooooh," he said. "Big man on campus."

I gave him half a smile.

"How about a stogie?" the whale called out to the pit boss, who motioned for the cigarette girl in the next pit.

I always felt sorry for cigarette girls. Their job was to look enticing in a short skirt and heels while carrying around a huge tray of cigars, cigarettes, and Tiparillos. A strap around the neck was meant to lighten the load, but I doubt it did any good.

She walked over to the whale. He dug around in her tray until he found what he wanted. She prepared it for him by snipping off the end. Then lit a match while he used his right to roll the cigar in the flame.

"You done?" I asked.

"Keep your shirt on," he said and blew out a puff. He looked the girl up and down, gave her a chip with his cigar hand, and returned to the table. "Wouldn't mind having one of those either," he said.

I ignored the comment.

Options were simple at this point. If you didn't feel your hand was strong enough, you could fold. If you liked your hand, or didn't like your hand, but could bluff, you could call, meaning you'd throw the same amount of chips on the pile as were just bet. If you really liked your hand, or were a master bluffer, you could raise the bet, meaning you threw in what was just bet, then threw in some more on top of it.

The cardigan folded. The military man stayed silent for a moment. He may have been waiting for a salute, I couldn't tell. He looked at the pot, then at his hands, then at the pot again before finally calling.

The whale was busy with his drink. He took a puff, blew the smoke out up above his head, then matched the bet, though he seemed in no hurry to do it. He wasn't looking at his cards and he wasn't watching the other players. In fact, at times he seemed lost in his own world—as if he forgot there was even a game going on. Perhaps this was his strategy. But quite frankly, he looked bored.

I threw three cards face down on the table in front of me. The cardigan chuckled.

"Something I can help you with?" I asked.

"I figured you were bluffing," he said. "Now I'm sure of it."

"Well, that's the name of the game, isn't it?" I asked. "People who can't bluff, fold."

That garnered me a stern look from the cardigan and a laugh from the whale.

Hollis took my three and dealt me three more. The military man took one card and the whale two.

A cocktail waitress came over and refreshed the whale's drink. She looked over at me with a raised eyebrow. I shook my head and she left.

My hand was looking up. Hollis had dealt me two jacks. If I'd kept the one I had, I'd have a full house about now. But I'd lost my crystal ball somewhere along the way, so I didn't do what I should have. Still, two pair wasn't bad, even if it was a low two. I threw two more chips into the pot to see if I could bluff my way into a win.

The military man was disappointed with his fifth card, I could see it in his eyes. He was probably going for that same straight the whale had gone for. Hoping lightning would strike twice. Why else would he throw in one card? A smart man would keep what he had and try to run a bluff. When lightning didn't strike, he folded.

"Looks like it's you and me," I said to the whale.

The whale's cards were laying face down on the table in front of him; he hadn't looked at them since he first placed them there. Instead, the big man looked over at me. A corner of his mouth raised slightly. His gaze was steady, but not harsh. He wasn't daring me to bet. In fact, he wasn't really even looking at me, as much as past me. Or maybe through me was the better word. This man wasn't a person uncomfortable with another man's eyes. No, he had no problem keeping my gaze, silently watching me.

He took two chips and placed them in the pot, which now totaled one hundred and forty-five dollars, a tidy little sum.

"I'll call your two," I said throwing in the chips, "and raise you two more."

He picked up two chips and tossed them in as well.

"No more bets," Hollis said.

I threw down my two pair. "They're not quite grown yet," I said. "But I'll play 'em just the same."

The whale laid down a pair of twos, then another pair of fours. I had him so far. That was until he added the other four. Full house.

We played several more hands, and before I knew it, an hour had passed. I wasn't playing to win. I was playing to watch. The whale looked around the pit, seemingly bored. He watched the pit bosses, the other dealers, even the players at times. He stared out the entrance doors and watched the people walking around. He paid attention to almost everything but the cards.

The cardigan won a couple, the military man won one or two, but the whale, even distracted, won the most. I found it interesting that his demeanor was the same, win or lose. He was happy when he won—and he won quite a bit—but he wasn't upset when he lost. He also took chances that most people wouldn't take. Sometimes they panned out, sometimes they didn't. And through it all, he drank. I had seen this once before—when a man wasn't playing with his own money.

I was about to lay down the next ante when a hand touched my shoulder.

"There you are," Lizzie said. "Where have you been hiding?"

I turned to look. Lizzie was still dressed in her red circle dress, with matching flats, gloves, and purse. "Hiding?" I repeated. "What makes you think I've been hiding?"

"Well, you haven't been here," she said, "so you must have been hiding." She slipped her hand from my shoulder to my back.

"I do have a life, you know."

"Pish posh," she said. She opened her purse and took out her lipstick and a small mirror. "Take me away from here, Maxie. Richey is boring me."

I presumed she meant the whale.

She flashed him a stern look as she applied her makeup. "And he's drinking again," she added. The sugar gone from her tone.

Richey raised his glass.

"How many of those have you had?" she asked and

snapped her purse shut.

"One more than I should, and several less than I will."

"Maybe you should slow down," she said.

"Maybe you should get bent," he countered. "You do your part, Ronnie, and I'll do mine. If it wasn't for me, you'd still be on Western Avenue."

She flashed him a look that would have made a button man cringe, then suddenly turned her attention back to me. "C'mon, Maxie, take me away from all this," she said, all sugar and spice.

That caught the whale's attention. "You the one been taking her around?" he asked.

"Yeah, that's me," I confirmed.

His head went cockeyed, like he was trying to place me. "Good for you," he finally said. "Why don't you take the skirt away from here? Show her a good time. Loosen her up a bit. She's tightly wound for a doxie."

I could feel the veins in my neck tighten. I stood slowly. "Maybe you should watch your tongue," I said.

The cardigan pushed his chair back, turned to slip out of it, and fell to the ground. He got up and skidded away, leaving his chips on the table.

"Maybe you should blow while you still can," the whale said.

Now my fist was tightening as well. I caught the pit boss out of the corner of my eye. He was shaking his head.

Lizzie took my arm. "C'mon, Maxie. Take me somewhere fun."

"Yeah. Go ahead, Maxie. Take her somewhere fun," the whale said.

Its moments like these that define a man. Is he willing to stand up for what is right or will he go cower in a corner? The whale was asking for a whack on the beak and I was just the rube to give it to him.

"They're just words," the military man said without looking up. "And words mean nothing. Nothing at all. That is, unless you let them."

"Stay out of this," the whale said.

The military man held up his hands in submission.

I stepped toward the whale, but then I thought about the Emerald Room and how well that had gone. I thought about all the times my father had told me I needed to learn to control my temper. I thought about my job, about Fingers, and Virginia, and that envelope in my vent. Then I placed my lid on my head, picked up my chips, and held out my arm, just like the nuns had taught me.

"Shall we?" I said to Lizzie.

She took my arm. "We shall."

NINE

LIZZIE WAS FAMISHED but also wanted to get away from the Sands, so I took her to the El Sombrero Café, for a little Mexican cuisine. The El Sombrero was a converted house, built in the 1930s when Las Vegas' neighbor to the east, Boulder City, was busy building a marvel that would eventually be known as the Hoover Dam. The house faced the railroad tracks, making its location, at the time, perfect for the up-and-coming village that would eventually become the boomtown of Las Vegas.

The adobe building had been in the hands of Clemente Griego for more than a decade, ever since he turned the place first into a taco-selling cantina, and, when that took off, a full-fledged restaurant. Though Clemente came to Las Vegas to nurse a broken heart, he eventually found love with his wife Emily. It was she who seated us.

The place was as small as one would expect a house

built in the '30s to be. The entire dining room consisted of six booths—three on each side of the room—and seven small tables in the center. All manner of Sombreros hung on the walls next to paintings of bullfighting and adobe buildings.

The restaurant was relatively empty, as it was far too late for lunch and much too early for dinner, except for three rowdy Tam O'Shanter-adorned men who occupied a booth toward the back. Emily showed us to a similar booth on the other side of the room.

She handed us two menus. "I will be back to take your orders," she said in a slight Spanish accent.

After she left our table, she headed to the wall and removed one of the sombreros from its peg. She walked over to the three men, the sombrero behind her back. "And who lost the bet this time?" she asked.

Two of the men pointed to the third. "He did," they said in unison.

"I am sorry, Gary," she said and placed the sombrero on his head.

The two others roared with laughter.

"What's going on there?" Lizzie asked while looking at the menu.

"Looks like Gary lost a bet," I said.

"A bet?" she asked. "What kind of bet?"

"I have no idea, but it appears the loser of said bet must have to wear a sombrero during dinner. I wouldn't be surprised if said loser was expected to pay for the entire meal as well."

"Men," Lizzie said. "Can't live with 'em, can't shoot 'em." She peeked over the top of the menu and flashed me a coy smile. It made me wonder if she'd tested that theory.

Emily returned to our table with three bowls. One

was filled with corn chips and the other with what she identified as Pico de Gallo. The third had salsa.

"Made it myself," she said.

Emily skirted off, giving us time to examine the menu a bit closer. Most of it was written in Spanish, of which my broken Italian provided no assistance.

"Can you read any of this?" I asked.

"Si," Lizzie said. "Mi abuela ere de España."

I looked at her blankly.

"My grandmother was from Spain."

"Really?" I asked. "Are there a lot of blondes in Spain?"

"Don't be a germ," she said. "A girl's hair can be any color she wants it to be."

That was fair.

"There was a little cantina back in Boston I used to go to," I said. "They had the best eggs and potatoes I've ever had."

"That's papas con huevos," Lizzie said.

"Then that's what I want."

When Emily returned, Lizzie ordered a cheese quesadilla and a Modelo Especial.

"What is that?" I asked.

"Mexican beer," Emily said.

"My grandfather used to drink it," Lizzie offered. "It was all they could get during prohibition."

"Interesting," I said.

"It's good. You should try it," she said.

"I'll take papas con hevos," I said, butchering the pronunciation. "And a Modelo..."

"Papas con huevos and Modelo Especial," Emily said, saving me from further bastardizing her native tongue before she turned and left.

Lizzie laughed. She took a chip from the dish, dipped it in the salsa, and took a bite. "Don't you speak another language?" she asked.

"Un po Italiano," I said.

"Well they're both Latin based, so it should be easy for you to pick up."

"I'll keep that in mind," I said, then joined her in the salsa. It sat on my tongue, punching my taste buds into submission with flaming fists. I coughed. My eyes began to water.

Lizzie laughed harder this time. "Too hot for you?" she asked.

Luckily, Emily arrived at just that moment with our two beers. I quickly downed about half of mine. "I'm gonna need another of these," I managed to cough out.

Emily nodded and left.

The boys must have been watching because they were laughing too. They raised their glasses to me. I followed suit, trying to regain my composure.

"So you're from Spain?" I asked when the heat finally died down.

"I'm from all over," she said.

"A gypsy?" I asked.

She looked at me with her ice-blue eyes. "Perhaps," she said.

"What did your father do for a living?"

"He was a pirate."

"I see. Broadsword, eye patch, the whole bit?"

"Something like that," she said.

"And your mother?"

Lizzie lowered her eyes and bit her bottom lip. "I

never knew my mother," she said. "She died when I was very young."

"I'm sorry to hear that," I said. It was not a memory I had intended to bring her. I decided to change the subject. "What was the jewelry store about?" I asked.

Her face lit up. She reached across the table and took my hands. "Oh, Maxie, don't be cross with me," she said. "Sometimes a girl just needs to have a little fun."

She gave me pouty lips.

"That why you're with Dorsey?" I asked.

She pulled her hands back and sat up straight. "I don't want to talk about him," she said.

I ignored her. "What do you even know about him?"

"What're *you* writing a book?" she asked.

"The casino likes to know a little about the people who come in loaded," I said.

"What's there to know?" she asked. "We met in California. He has money and he wanted to have a time in Las Vegas, so I tagged along."

"Not what you thought it would turn out to be?" I asked.

Her gaze fell to the table and she shook her head slowly. She picked the napkin from her lap, opened it, and began folding it anew. "He drinks far too much," she said, and the ice in her eyes darkened. "And he's not very nice."

"Why don't you just leave him?" I asked.

She didn't answer for the longest time. Then she suddenly looked up with a bright smile. "You ever think of marrying?" she asked as she smoothed out the napkin on her lap.

"Not me," I said. "I'm confirmed."

"And you have no girl?" she asked.

"No one to speak of," I lied.

"Well, the girls don't know what they're missing."

Just then Emily came with our food and another beer. As Lizzie nibbled on her quesadilla, I thought about women like her, ones who grabbed for that brass ring. Searching for something they were unlikely to find; something that even if found, would surely produce bitter fruit. Lizzie was seeing that now. So was I.

"Are you going to be in terrible trouble?" she asked suddenly.

"Trouble?" I repeated.

"With the jewelry store."

"Does it matter?" I asked.

"Of course it matters, Maxie," she said in a way that almost made me believe her. "I don't want you to be in trouble."

I assured her I'd be fine and that the store would likely drop charges. It didn't seem to surprise her.

"Is that because of your job?"

"At the Sands? Could be, but it's more likely they'll see I was being played as the sap."

She reached across the table and put her hands on mine. "Oh, Maxie, don't be like that. Don't let's be mean."

I patted her hand and forced a smile.

"What was that crack about Western Avenue?" I asked.

She pulled back her hands. Her face hardened. "His little joke," she said. "He likes to compare me to a happy lady. He thinks he's clever."

"And Ronnie?"

Her eyes grew big for just an instant and she stiffened, but to her credit, she recovered quickly. "Oh, it's just a name he likes to call me. It doesn't mean anything." She sat quietly for a moment, then asked with a smile, "What were you doing at the poker table?"

"Looking for you," I said.

"You always play poker when you're looking for someone?"

"Not always," I admitted. "But it's often a good place to start."

"It looked like you knew what you were doing," she said. "You play much?"

"Some," I said. "When my pockets get lonely."

"And they let you gamble there?"

"Sure," I said. "As long as I don't win."

That brought back the smile. I preferred it.

When our meal was finished and our beers downed, Lizzie and I climbed back into my Roadmaster. As I brought the engine to life, Lizzie leaned over and kissed me. It was a kiss from deep inside her. The kind you gave to someone you didn't know, someone who would keep your inner-most secrets. The kind you gave when you just needed to feel something. I didn't mind.

When it was done, Lizzie brought her fingers to her mouth and slowly wiped them across her lips. Just as she had done before. "I liked that," she said.

I put the car in gear as Lizzie moved herself closer and leaned her head on my shoulder. It felt better than it should have. I drove her back to the Sands, parking in my spot. We sat there for a moment before finally getting out. I closed the door behind her and escorted her inside like a proper gentleman.

Some gentleman, I thought.

Lizzie suddenly stopped and turned to me. "Take me somewhere tonight," she said. "Somewhere there's music and people dance."

"You know I can't do that," I said. "What would Dorsey say?"

Her face grew stern, like she had eaten a distasteful meal or a rotten piece of fruit. "People like him don't last very long," she said. "Why does it matter what he thinks?"

"Because this isn't just a tête-à-tête," I said. "I work here."

Lizzie pulled her arm from mine. "And I'm just an assignment," she said coarsely.

"It's not that..." But before I could finish, she slapped my face and stormed off.

TEN

I STOOD THERE for a moment, rubbing my cheek. That girl had a right Marciano would have envied. A bellman came over and inquired as to my status. I assured him everything was fine. "Happens all the time," I admitted. I went over to the lobby and picked up the house phone.

"Mr. Abbandandolo's office," I said to the PBX operator. She connected me and when Fingers answered, I filled him in on all that had happened, including the slap to the face. He got much more enjoyment out of it than I had. I told him I might be hard to find for the rest of the night, but would check in with him in the morning.

"You'd better check back with me later," he said. "This palooka's winning and I want to keep him on the table as long as possible. You may have to take the skirt dancing after all."

Oh, goodie, I thought, but there was little I could do

but agree. After I hung up with Fingers, I fished the card Keys had given me out of my pocket and asked PBX to connect me. This time he answered.

"What'da ya know, Joe?" he asked.

"I'm not sure who Joe is, but if your offer to go with me to buy a saxophone still holds, I'm in."

"Max!" he exclaimed. "I knew you'd call. You want a sax? It's eggs in the coffee, man!"

I hoped that was a good thing.

We arranged to meet at Garwood Van's Music Land in Francisco Square across from the Sahara Hotel and Casino, just down the highway from the Sands. I was there in less than fifteen minutes. Keys showed about ten minutes later in a bright green, ragtop Bel Air with whitewall tires.

He came over to me in his cheaters and pork pie hat and slapped his hand into mine. "You're going to love this place," he said. "It's owned by none other than Garwood Van."

The name didn't register and it showed.

"Don't tell me you don't know who Garwood Van is," he exclaimed. "Man, have you been living under a rock? Garwood has the best band in town. He ran the show at the El Rancho and The Last Frontier. How do you not know Garwood?"

"I haven't been here that long," I admitted. "I haven't had a chance to tap into the music scene."

"Come with me," Keys said.

I followed him inside the building. It was a typical music store. Bins lined the walls, filled with records separated alphabetically by artist. Some bins contained LPs, while others held 45s. There were also bins of sheet music and instruments hung from hooks high on every wall. A drum set was located in one corner, surrounded by keyboards and two upright pianos.

I moved toward the saxophones. There were altos, tenors, and sopranos but no baris. That didn't surprise me. Baris were heavy, not something you hung on a wall. He had the three major brands: Conn, King, and Selmer. The Mark VI immediately caught my eye. I was about to ask if one could be taken down from the wall when a bright-eyed man with a leading chin and a tight haircut came forcefully from the back room.

"Vinny 'Keys' Collins!" he bellowed. "You got some nerve coming into this store. Why don't you drop dead twice?"

"What, and look like you?" Keys said.

There they stood, toe to toe, each refusing to give way. Keys in a Gaucho-style shirt with brown sleeves and matching slacks. His opponent in a smart suit with a watercolor tie. Just as I was wondering if we had entered into the wrong establishment, the two men threw their arms around each other. I allowed myself a breath.

"Keys Collins. Well, a ring-a-ding-ding!"

"Garwood Van," Keys said as the men separated. "You're looking good."

"Not as good as you," Garwood said.

"I can't complain."

"Oh? Why's that?"

"It ain't allowed," Keys said. "It ain't allowed."

They laughed.

"How long you been in town?" Garwood asked.

"Couple a weeks," Keys said.

"What brings you to our neck of the woods?"

"Music, man. It's always the music."

"It ain't always the music," Garwood said. "Sometimes it's the dames."

Keys grinned broadly. "You know me. I ain't gonna argue with you on that one." Keys turned to me. "This is my friend Max. He needs a saxophone. It's been a while since he played, but his chops are fantastic and he's lookin' to get back in the saddle. Sat in with us the other night over at Bootlegger."

"Pleased to meet you," Garwood said and stuck out his hand.

I took it. His grip was firm. "Likewise," I said.

"You playin' with the Five and Dimes again?" he asked Keys.

Keys nodded.

He turned back to me. "You look like a Selmer man," he said.

I raised a curious brow.

"I noticed you eyeballing that Mark VI," he said. "Would you like to try it out?" I told him I would, and he had one of his employees take it down off the wall. He handed it to me. "The action on the keys is great," he said. "They relocated and resized the tone holes, changed the design of the bore, and moved the key grips."

He handed the sax to me. "Try that on for size," he said. "This is likely the best sax ever built. Of course, King is also popular with those who venture into jazz, but I have to admit, I'm kind of partial to Selmer myself."

I played with the keys a bit, bouncing my fingers up and down. Garwood was right, the action was tight but comfortable. The pads closed nicely and the pearl on the keys welcomed my fingers. Even without the neck strap, the instrument felt good in my hands; it had a nice balance, one that transported me to my youth. Back to the days when I was first learning to play. When I was trying to impress a girl I had no chance with.

Another employee approached. He had on dungarees with the cuffs rolled up and a button-down shirt that was apparently missing the top two buttons. "You layin' down the hustle?" he asked Keys.

It was twice I'd heard that in the last two days.

Keys nodded and the two men walked away. Garwood either didn't notice or didn't care. "You got a mouthpiece?" he asked.

I admitted that I didn't and told him I couldn't remember what mouthpiece I had used. I played a student Conn. It had a good sound, but nothing to get excited about. Instead of putting their money into a better sax, my parents put it into a better mouthpiece and it made a world of difference. When I was older and had laid the instrument back in its case for good, it, along with the mouthpiece, went to a cousin who wanted to play. I never saw the thing again.

"Try this one." Garwood handed me a Vandoren. "This is as good as it gets," he said. "I met Eugène Van Doren in Paris. He was the clarinetist for the Paris opera and the Colonne Orchestra. Makes a damn fine mouthpiece and reed. Speaking of which, what number reed do you use?"

"I played a five, but I doubt I could vibrate that now," I said. We agreed on a three. Garwood pulled a reed out of a pack and handed it to me. I put the reed into my mouth to soften it, then attached it to the mouthpiece with the ligature. I put the thing to my lips, bit down, and blew. I went up and down some scales and then played a piece I had memorized as a kid, but couldn't remember the name.

Keys returned. His eyes as red as a woman's lips.

"Let's head over to the ivories," Garwood said, "and jam a bit."

We walked to the corner of the room. Keys took a keyboard and Garwood sat at one of the uprights. "Just play," Garwood said. "We'll jump in when it feels right."

I let the music guide me. Playing whatever came to my head, and eventually my heart. At some point, Keys and Garwood joined in, but I don't remember when. The employee came back as well and took a position at the trap set and then we really had a jam session going. Customers came in. Many stood and listened. Some cheered us on. We played for the better part of an hour before finally winding down.

"Man, that was cookin' with gas!" Keys said. Garwood agreed. Who was I to argue? Truth be told, they carried me, but I didn't mind. When you've got musicians the caliber of those two, you just hold on and ride the wave as far as it goes.

"What do you think?" Garwood asked.

"Nice sound, great action, it's a good horn," I said. "How much?"

"Two bills," Garwood said. "Case, mouthpiece, and neck strap included. Heck, I'll even throw in a box of reeds."

"One seventy-five," I said.

He rubbed his chin for a moment, stalling. But I'd played too many hands of poker to lose this one.

"I can't do that," he finally said. "Not enough skin in it for me."

I unhooked the instrument and pulled the strap from around my neck. "Well, thanks for letting me try it out, anyway," I said and extended the instrument to him. He didn't take it. I didn't expect him to. A good salesman kept the merchandise in the customer's hand as long as possible. The more it sat there, the more it felt like it belonged, and the harder it was to give back. I laid the sax carefully on the piano bench next to him.

Garwood stood.

Keys kept silent.

"It was a pleasure meeting you," I said. "How much do I owe you for the reed?"

Garwood gave me a sideways grin. "One eighty," he offered, "And you can keep the reed."

"Throw in some sheet music and I'll take it," I said.

Twenty minutes later I walked out the front door, the proud owner of a new Selmer alto saxophone and several sheets of music.

Keys lit up. "That was pretty impressive," he said and took a drag. He offered me one, but I declined. "Where'd you learn how to negotiate?"

"I occasionally play the Bees," I said.

"Blackjack?" he asked.

"Poker," I responded. "Blackjack's for mugs."

Keys took another puff. "You're an interesting man, Max Rossi," he said. "Very interesting." He took his last puff, then tossed the cigarette to the ground. "You hungry?" he asked.

"I could eat," I said.

"Know a good place?"

"I'm kind of partial to the Garden Room at the Sands."

"That's where you work, right?" Keys asked and headed to his car. "I'll follow you."

ELEVEN

LESS THAN TEN minutes later we were parked in front of the Sands, I in my spot and Keys in valet. We went inside, headed to the Garden Room, and settled into a booth under a painting of Marlene Dietrich, near the copper boiler, right in front of a row of exotic-looking plants. I liked the place, partially because of the garden-like ambiance and partially because all my meals were comped.

I laid my lid on the seat beside me. Keys laid his cheaters on the table but kept his lid in place, receiving a stern glare from the waitress. It didn't affect him. The Garden Room had a nice à la carte menu, complete with French sardines, jellied madrilène, and borscht with sour cream. The Mexican I had for lunch was still knocking around in my gut, so I decided to go with something a little more traditional. I ordered a club sandwich and opted for coleslaw instead of fried potatoes. Keys ordered the hamburger deluxe and asked the waitress to slap a piece of cheese on top of it.

He pulled a smoke from his pack and lit up, then took in the view. "So this is where you work," he said.

"This is where I work," I confirmed.

"And what is it you said you do?"

"Oh, a little of this, a little of that."

He laughed. "Very informative. What are you, a secret agent?"

It was my turn to laugh. "No," I said. "Nothing like that. I just do whatever needs to be done. For example, today I had to take a butter and egg man's doll out to lunch. In fact, I've had to show her around the town for a couple of days now."

"She a looker?"

I thought it a strange question. "Does it matter?" I asked.

"Of course it matters. If she's the cat's meow, at least you got something to occupy your eyes."

There was that.

"She's flighty, and more than a handful," I said. "No duck soup with this one. All I've gotten for my troubles is a rap sheet and a slap across the beak."

"Ain't that a bite," Keys exclaimed.

Indeed, I thought.

The waitress brought our meals. I was still feeling the sting of Lizzie's slap, so I ordered a manhatten to make it dust out. Keys ordered rye, straight up.

"You said you played the Bees," Keys said while smacking enough ketchup onto his burger to pass for a crime scene. "You any good at it?"

"Passable," I said. "Better than some, worse than others."

Keys took a bite of his burger. "Do you ever give a

straight answer?" he asked with a full mouth.

"I guess that depends on the question," I said. "What is it you do?" I asked, then bit into my own sandwich.

Keys swallowed. "A little of this, a little of that," he said.

"Touché," I said. Then added, "You can't make it on jazz and selling those sticks of tea."

He grinned. "You noticed that, did you?"

"Pretty hard to miss," I said. "So, how do you get by?"

"Gigs don't pay the rent, that's for sure," Keys admitted. "But there are other ways to make scratch."

"Such as?"

"I don't know you well enough to answer that question," he said and took another bite.

"What do you need to know about me?" I said. I told him I was an open book, but forgot to mention that some of the pages had been torn out.

"You mobbed up?" he asked out of the blue.

"What makes you ask that?" I countered.

"You're Italian, you've got a Boston accent, you work in a casino I've been told is mob run, and you never give a straight answer to a question."

"Occupational hazard," I assured him.

"Then you are mob?"

I shook my head. "Dipped my toe in once, but it wasn't for me."

"I didn't think they let you out once you were in," Keys said.

"I was never official. Just a junior mobster in training. Never got the merit badge."

A cocktail waitress showed with our drinks. I thanked her and laid a nugget on her tray.

Keys watched her walk all the way to the door. "They sure know how to dress here," he said, then added, "That kitten with you the other night, the one with the gams, she your gal?"

That's twice I'd been asked about the status of my relationship in one day. I'd lied the first time. "We spend time together," I said. "Nothing steady." Looks like I could tell the truth after all. Who knew?

"I bet she's no flat tire," he said.

"Awful forward of you, isn't it?"

"Let's not get bent out of shape," Keys said. "I didn't mean anything by it. She's just keen is all."

I let the comment go. Keys was probably right; he didn't mean anything by it. I was too jumpy about our relationship anyway. I didn't know where it was going and, more importantly, I wasn't sure I knew where I wanted it to go just yet.

We finished our respective meals and each shared another drink. Keys lit his next cigarette. He placed his arm over the top of the bench and leaned back.

"Seriously," I said. "How do you get by?"

"OPM," he offered.

"You got me there," I admitted.

"Other people's money," he clarified. "Why spend your own when you can spend someone else's?" he said with a grin.

I was beginning to think he'd get along nicely with Lizzie. "So you're a grifter?" I asked.

"A fakaloo artist?" he asked. "No, nothing like that. I don't take advantage of people."

"Not according to your card."

Keys let out a snort. "Aw, that's just for fun. Makes people remember you. See, it worked."

"I'm not sure it's necessary," I said. "You're pretty hard to forget."

Keys tipped his hat and nodded his thank you. "You really looking for a side hustle?" he asked.

"Sure," I said.

"Think you can book a room, maybe a suite?"

I was about to answer when a man in a suit large enough for three people came to our table, cigar in hand.

"There you are," Fingers said and motioned for me to follow him.

I climbed out of the booth, replaced my lid, excused myself, and followed him over to the entrance of the restaurant.

"Change of plans," he said casually. "You're taking Averill out tonight."

"Why the change?" I asked.

"This Dorsey's having a run of luck. Big pots. Great money for the house. You keep her away, so he can stay on the tables."

"And what am I supposed to do with her?"

He handed me a twenty. "Wine and dine her. Take her dancing. Do whatever you want, as long as you keep her out of the casino tonight."

I gave him a reluctant nod.

"You made any progress on the Highwaymen?" he asked. "They hit the El Rancho last night."

"What time?"

"Who knows," Fingers said. "Could have been nine, could have been ten; could have been three in the morning. We only ever find out when they do the count."

The count Fingers referred to was the daily tally of all the money that came in and went out of the casino. There was a detailed, fastidious accounting of every table game, as well as every change booth, slot machine, and the casino cage itself—minus the skim, of course. A nickel wasn't moved two inches without the casino knowing about it.

I was surprised Fingers knew where these Highwaymen had hit. Mobsters aren't well known for sharing information. Something bad happens to another casino, too bad. It just means less competition.

"How are you finding out?" I asked.

Fingers pointed at me, cigar in hand. "You just worry about your end," he said. "And let me worry about mine."

"Can't do much when I'm babysitting," I said. "It'd help to have someone to talk to. Someone with a bit more knowledge. If you've got a connection, you might want to share."

Fingers took a deep drag and mulled it around for a bit, to see how it looked in the mirror, before continuing. "My goomah's cousin is a pit boss there," he said, then added. "Name's Preston. But that's just between you and me, got it?"

I assured him I did.

"You won't get anything from him," Fingers said. "He's an idiot. I've already spoken to him and got bupkis. He knows as much about gambling as I do about eating leafy greens. How he got that job I'll never know."

"Mind if I try?"

"Do as you please," Fingers said. He turned to leave, then suddenly stopped. "By the way," he said. "I've booked you a room here indefinitely. I want you staying on property until this whole thing is resolved. That going to be a problem?"

"No," I said. "I'll pack an overnight bag."

When I returned, Keys had killed a second smoke and was on to his third.

"Good news?" he asked.

I sat heavily in the booth. "Hardly," I said. "Looks like babysitting duty again tonight."

"Great! Why don't you two join me at the Round up Room?"

"The Round up Room?" I asked.

"At the El Rancho, where Nancy dances. I can get Jimmy to hook us up with some tickets."

"OPM?" I asked.

"Hey, man. A comp's a comp. They give them away like candy around here."

He had a point. "All right," I said. I didn't know what I was going to do with Lizzie anyway, and she did ask to go somewhere there was dancing.

"Perfect," Keys said. He grabbed his cheaters and slid out of the booth. "I've got to run. Got some things to do before the show." He shook my hand and turned to leave. "See you around nine?"

I nodded and he left. It was then I realized he hadn't paid for his meal.

TWELVE

I NEEDED TO get home and pack a bag for my extended stay, but first I had a stop to make. Virginia and I had spoken about going out after her last show tonight and I needed to tell her I couldn't make it, so I headed to the Copa Room. The place was being set up for the night, servers laying white cloths on tables, decorating them with lights and flowers and silverware for the first show, the dinner show.

A man in dark black slacks and a matching turtleneck stood on stage, yelling at hands, telling them how he wanted the lights to be set. I slipped onto the stage. He glanced at me, jerked a thumb toward the backstage, and advised me not to be long. I headed to the dressing room and found Thelma, the wardrobe lady, busily making last-minute touchups to the new costumes.

She looked up at me through the tops of her bifocals. "Virginia's inside," she said.

I opened the dressing room door to a plethora of mostly naked ladies. They yelled, and I yanked the door closed.

Thelma laughed. "Maybe try knocking first," she said.

That would have been useful information.

After a few minutes, a dancer I knew as Cat poked her head out the door. "Oh, it's you, Max," she said. "I'll get Virginia."

When Virginia showed, she was wearing a silk robe that hit her mid-thigh. It was a beautiful thigh at that— one of which I was growing very fond. She was thick with stage makeup, ready for the show. Eyelashes that almost poked me. Hair all done up. I wasn't much of a greasepaint guy. I preferred my women au naturel. The way the good Lord intended.

She pulled out a smoke, and I lit it for her. "Can't make it tonight," I said.

"Oh?"

"Work," I continued. "It can't be helped. I've been tasked with taking the whale's moll out again. Get her away, so he can stay on the tables."

"I thought he was playing poker," Virginia said.

"He is," I assured her.

"Then they make money off him either way," she said. "So why do they need you to occupy her time?"

I wasn't sure if she was seeking clarification or testing me. "The longer he stays at the tables, the more money they make," I said. "They don't want him to go anywhere and she's not one content to watch the Bees."

She pursed her lips.

"Rain check?" I asked.

Virginia leaned in and kissed me on the cheek. "No

funny business," she warned and sent me on my way.

As I turned to leave, Thelma looked up and tapped her right cheek. I pulled my handkerchief from my pocket and wiped off the lipstick Virginia had planted there. "Thanks," I said. "You're a doll."

Thirty minutes later I was back in my house packing for a vacation at the Sands—hoping this one would go better than the last. As I folded my clothes into the suitcase, I thought about the Highwaymen and wondered just how I was going to work my way into a group no one seemed to know anything about. I also wondered what side hustle Keys had in mind. The envelope in the vent offered no useful suggestions. My father was big on planning and he would have advised me to create a plan and then stick to it.

The first thing he did when he was called in was to assess the situation. How bad it was, what needed to be done, and how quickly. These were the first questions he taught me to ask. Once you had the answers, you could develop a step-by-step course of action and then implement it. Only problem was, I wasn't cleaning up a mess that had already happened. I was supposed to stop the mess from happening in the first place. All I knew so far was that this group of cheats had hit the El Rancho and I needed to stop them before they hit the Sands. It wasn't much to go on, but at least I had a place to start.

I drove back to the Sands, checked into my room, and made myself comfortable. I freshened up and would have put on fancier duds, but I wasn't in the mood for dapper—this was business, not pleasure.

When I was all spick and span, I headed to Lizzie's suite. I decided to walk outside in the manicured garden area, which, true to its name, was complete with all manner of foliage, flowers, shrubs, roses, palm trees, and olive trees. I liked olive trees, not because they produced the national fruit of Italy, but because while many considered them ugly, I felt they had their own unique beauty.

The cabana buildings, which were simply hotel rooms on two stories, surrounded the garden, blocking out the desert and helping to provide a feeling of being in an oasis. At night there was enough mood lighting to make even the least amorous couple fall for cupid's arrow. Every olive tree, palm tree, and bush had its own light shining upward from the ground. Even the pool was lit at night. It gave the place a surreal feeling and must have cost a small fortune to keep lit. But that was none of my business.

All the buildings at the Sands were named for racetracks—not oilfields, as one might expect from a man who reportedly made his fortune in Texas tea. Likewise, all the suites were named for racehorses. Lizzie's was Whirlaway, the wild chestnut stallion that won the Triple Crown in '41 and the Travers Stakes that same year—the first and only horse to have ever won both.

As I headed down the hallway, I passed a security officer dressed as a policeman. It was intentional on the part of the hotel. "All quiet on the Western front?" I asked.

"Who's askin'?"

I pulled some lettuce from my pocket and held out a single. "The Fuller Brush Man," I said. I could have told him I worked there, but why chance it? I figured the fewer people knew about me, the better. You never knew when you might have to look into the actions of an employee. It would help if they didn't know I was the house dick.

He took the bill. I handed him another.

"You heard much coming from this suite?" I asked, motioning toward Whirlaway.

"Not now," he said. "But earlier, yeah."

I was intrigued. "Like what?" I asked.

"They got into quite a row," he said. "Pretty common with them. He's a yeller, but she gives as good as she gets."

"Could you hear what the argument was about?" I asked.

He hesitated. I passed him another bill.

He shook his head. "Not really. That suite's a big one, so it doesn't come much through the door. I only listen enough to tell if someone needs help. Otherwise, it ain't any business of mine what couples do."

He paused a moment, looked down the hall, then leaned into me. "I can tell you one thing, though. There's plenty of action coming in and going out."

"Action?" I asked.

He moved a little closer. "Girls mainly," he said a bit softer. "You know, like the roundheels that used to be down there in Block 16 before they ran 'em out in '51."

It's not that it was uncommon for high rollers to get associated with the ladies of the evening—this was Vegas after all. However, when that high roller had already brought a dame of his own with him, well, that was a zucchini of a different color.

"Just doxies?" I asked.

"No, sometimes there are others, mostly men."

I was beginning to wonder if Dorsey and Lizzie were having the kind of parties that would have made Diana Dors proud. I thanked the officer, handed him a single, and waited until he made his way down the hall before I pressed the bell to the suite.

Lizzie answered with her usual bright smile and no sign of having been in an earlier clash. She was adorned in a full-length skirt and matching off the shoulder top that would have made the nuns blush, pulling my eyes to a place they had no business going. A polite man would have closed his gaping pie hole. I wasn't a polite man. The top and bottom were separated by a thick belt, but not much else. Baubles adorned each wrist—though there wasn't a panther head in sight—and both ears were decorated with a gold loop.

Her blonde hair was all done up in a large wave over her left eye, ending in a curve around the ear. The right side was pulled back. Noticing my eyes, she wrapped a cardigan over her bare shoulders.

"Better?" she asked.

It wasn't the word I would have used.

She pulled on a pair of gloves and produced a wide-brimmed hat seemingly out of nowhere. "Where are you taking me?" she asked as she positioned the hat in place.

"We're headed for the Round up Room at the El Rancho."

Lizzie looked at me sharply. "The El Rancho?" she repeated. "Why there? I wanted you to take me someplace where there's dancing."

"Then you are in luck," I said. "The Dice Girls are putting on a show especially for us. Dancing, dancing, and more dancing."

"Pish posh," she said. "I meant for us to dance. Take me somewhere else."

"No can do," I countered. "Arrangements have already been made. We are to meet a friend of mine."

She raised an eyebrow. "What's her name?"

"Keys," I said.

"Silly name for a girl."

"Luckily, he's no skirt," I said.

Lizzie leaned in. She placed her hands under my lapels and looked up at me with her ice-blue eyes and ruby lips. "Oh, Maxie," she said. "Let's not go there. Take me somewhere else." She pouted. "Please?"

I knew right then and there I was going to be in trouble before the night was through.

THIRTEEN

TWENTY MINUTES LATER we pulled into valet. The El Rancho wasn't nearly as fancy as the Sands, but it was also more than ten years it's elder. According to Vegas legend, businessman Tom Hull was traveling from California to Las Vegas in 1940 along Highway 91 when his car suddenly became difficult to steer. He pulled over to the side, got out, and found he had a flat tire. As Hull waited for help, he couldn't help but notice the number of cars passing along the highway. Hull owned a successful chain of resorts in California, called El Rancho, and the numerous cars gave him an idea. A year later, the El Rancho Vegas was born.

Though "Vegas" was officially part of the name, most people referred to the place simply as the El Rancho. It was just down Highway 91 from the Sands, near San Francisco Street, not terribly far from Garwood Van's. The main building looked like one might expect a casino named "Rancho" to look. That is, like a guest house on a ranch complete with a windmill tower. A wooden split rail fence served as a barrier between the casino and the highway. Like the Sands, The El Rancho's 220 hotel rooms were spread out on the back of the property. However, unlike the Sands, they were nowhere near the casino, and the grounds between the casino and the hotel rooms were no oasis.

The El Rancho was also one of the few places in Vegas where the mob hadn't yet established a foothold, though I'm sure they'd tried. Hopefully, the place had fire insurance.

I handed the attendant a couple of bones and told him to watch the paint, then I walked over to Lizzie's side and opened the door for her. I hadn't really noticed her legs before, but as she swept them out in her long skirt I got a brief look at her calves and ankles. They were a nice pair and did well to compliment her heels.

Lizzie seemed off from the moment we arrived. She pulled one of those thin cigarettes the ladies smoke from her purse and asked for a light. I had to chase the end with my match.

"You okay?" I asked.

"Certainly," she said. "Why wouldn't I be?"

I wanted to say, "Because you just got into a knock-down, drag-out with Richie," but thought better of it. She had protested the destination the entire way there, though I wasn't sure why. And just as I was about to give in, she relented and decided dancing girls would be a sufficient compromise. She clutched her purse under her arm, adjusted her hat, then took my arm as we entered.

The Western theme continued inside the place, ceilings constructed of heavy timber, wrought iron chandeliers, wood-paneled walls. Even the employees were decked out in Western garb. Every moment I was there, I expected someone to yell out "yippee ki-yay!"

Lizzie seemed oblivious to the scenery, concerning

herself only with the destination. I tried to slow as we passed the pits, but she pulled me tightly to keep me on course. When we got to the back of the barn, Keys was waiting for us. He was dressed in pleated slacks and a white short-sleeve shirt with the sleeves rolled to make them even higher. He left the top two buttons open and the collar stiff in the back. He was also missing his tie and lid. It was becoming the new trend in men's fashion. I didn't take to it. Give me a classic broadcloth sack suit, tie, matching square, and Stetson any day. At least he was holding the suit coat he needed for the show.

"Well, cast an eyeball on this pair," he said.

As he was prone to do, Keys slapped his hand into mine. I made the introductions. "Lizzie, this is Vinny Collins, but you can call him Keys. Everybody else does."

Keys took Lizzie's hand and held it high, inviting her to take a spin. Lizzie complied. "How'd you get a Dolly like this to hang out with you?" he asked.

"She came with the suit," I said, and received a slap on the arm for my trouble.

"A feisty one," Keys said. "I like that."

Lizzie pulled back her hand and smiled impatiently. "Why are we standing out here?" she asked. "Don't we have reservations?"

A true high roller's gal. Used to waiting her turn.

Keys pulled a smoke from his own pack and lit it. "Jimmy came through just fine," he said. "Our names are on a list with the maître d'."

"Then shall we?" Lizzie said and moved to the entrance of the showroom.

I shrugged and followed. Keys slipped on his jacket.

Moments later we were front row in the Round up Room watching a bevy of dancers sporting dice-shaped hats and cuffs, each sitting on a large die and kicking a firm leg high in the air. They were no Copa Girls, but enjoyable all the same.

Keys leaned over to us. "This is their opening act," he whispered. "Nancy's second from the right."

"Nancy?" Lizzie questioned.

"A friend's girl," I said.

It was at just that moment that Nancy looked over and noticed us sitting front row. She flashed us a performer's smile. I nodded and smiled back. Lizzie scooted her chair closer to mine and took hold of my arm. The girls stood and repositioned themselves behind their dice, this time putting a stockinged leg atop of the thing as they continued their routine. And just as Nancy glanced over a second time, Lizzie planted one on my cheek. Nancy's eyes widened.

I turned to Lizzie. "What gives?" I said.

"Oh don't be a wet rag," she countered. "I saw how she looked at you."

I was about to answer when the waitress came to take our order. "Two-drink minimum," she said, bending down so as not to obstruct the view.

I ordered two manhattans, Keys ordered two ryes straight up, and Lizzie ordered something called a gin and sin. Trouble was definitely brewing.

When the girls came out for their second number, Lizzie had moved close enough for me to count her as an accessory. She had downed the first drink and was working handily on the second. I was nursing my first and feeling not at all comfortable. Every time I tried to move her, Lizzie found her way back.

The stage was much smaller than the one in the Copa Room, barely enough room for the eight dancers. Nancy had the end position, and it impressed me how close she came to the edge of the stage without looking down. She came so close, in fact, that at one point several ladies gasped. Lizzie laughed.

The waitress came by and Lizzie ordered another drink.

"You might want to slow down," I said.

"Oh pish posh," she said, batting the air with her hand.

Keys was no help. "Let the lady drink," he said. "She isn't hurting anyone."

My cross look had little effect on him.

Lizzie turned to Keys. "I like the way you think," she said. "What do you do?"

"Oh, a little of this, a little of that," Keys said, giving me a wink.

Great, now I was being quoted.

"I'm a bum with one redeeming feature," Keys said. "I know my way around a keyboard."

"It's true," I added. "It's how he got his moniker."

"You can make a living doing that?" Lizzie asked.

"You can. If you know the secret," Keys said.

"And just what's the secret?" Lizzie asked.

He leaned over and whispered something into her ear.

"Interesting," Lizzie said, then took another drink and cozied back into me.

The Dice Girls danced, the audience applauded, and Lizzie kept drinking. By the time the show ended, Lizzie was feeling her oats. When the room emptied, we made our way out as well. I was genuinely surprised at how well Lizzie moved on her feet. She was standing so close to me a beam of light couldn't have peeked through, but she wasn't using me as a crutch. She was just holding on tightly.

"What shall we do now?" Keys asked.

"How about we head to the tables," I offered.

Lizzie protested. "Oh, no. Not the tables. I get enough of that with Richie."

"Not much else to do in a casino," I said.

Lizzie pushed herself up and leaned into my ear. "Well we don't have to stay here," she whispered.

An employee dressed like he had just come off the set of Howdy Doody appeared out of nowhere and approached Keys. He was the nervous type, holding a stiff arm downward and itching it with his other hand. His face was flushed and he seemed unable to stand still.

"I need to talk to you," he said to Keys. His words came out heavy, tinged with urgency.

"This ain't a good time," Keys said. He was talking to the man, but he wasn't looking at him.

The employee stepped closer. "There's been a problem," he said. He glanced over to us briefly, then quickly returned his attention to Keys. "With the horse," he said.

Keys flashed an awkward smile. It was the first time I'd seen him nervous.

"Go help the man with his horse," Lizzie said. "I'm going to powder my nose and then Maxie's going to take me away from here."

Lizzie kissed me on the cheek and headed to the restroom. I looked at Keys. "You'd better go before he itches his arm off," I said.

"On the flip side, then," Keys said and headed off with the employee.

While Lizzie was in the restroom, I headed over to the tables. The stage wasn't the only thing smaller in the place, the casino was easily half the size of the Sands. The pits consisted of six or seven tables, and there weren't many pits. I walked around, looking at name tags, hoping to find one that said Preston. Luck struck in the third pit where a man bearing such a tag was watching a lively game of craps.

On the table next to him, a male dealer, dressed in the same Howdy Doody attire, clapped his hands and held them up, wiggling his fingers. Preston looked at the man and nodded as a female dealer replaced him. The male dealer headed in my direction, following a line of other like-minded fellows heading to what I assumed was the employee area. I pulled a buck from my pocket, folded it tightly in my hand, and headed him off.

"Excuse me," I said.

"Yes, sir, how can I help you?"

"I was wondering if you could tell me when Preston gets off."

The dealer looked at me curiously. "It's okay," I said and held out my hand. "Name's Fuller."

The dealer took my hand. His eyes signaled that he had found the offering.

"I'm a cousin, just in from the east," I continued. "I want to surprise him."

"He's off at midnight, Mr. Fuller," the dealer said.

I thanked him, then reminded him that mum was the word. He agreed and shot off to join his compadres. I turned to find Lizzie behind me.

"You were not where I left you," she said.

"I have a wandering soul."

"C'mon," she said, pulling my arm. "You promised to take me away from here."

"I made no such promise," I said.

She pulled herself so close that her lips were inches from my ear. "Take me home and let's have some fun," she said, then took my earlobe between her teeth.

Rossi's Gamble

Trouble had come to town.

FOURTEEN

I DECIDED A bit of fresh air was in order, so I took the top down before we left and secured our hats in the trunk. Lizzie seemed to enjoy the night air. She slid herself around so her legs were on the seat, then lifted my arm and wrapped it around her as we turned right out of the lot.

"Just look at all the stars," she said. "Twinkling up there in the sky."

"It's probably a better idea that I keep my eyes on the road," I said.

"Oh, Maxie, you're no romantic at all."

"Said the woman who hitched a ride with a rich man to Las Vegas." It wasn't a particularly nice thing to say, but I wasn't in a particularly nice mood. Babysitting was not only growing tiresome, it was keeping me from my real task—finding the Highwaymen.

"It's such a delightful night that I'm choosing to ignore you," Lizzie said.

I ran the Roadmaster down Highway 91, following the posted speed signs, and headed for the Sands. The desert was peaceful at night, almost serene. But it was a deceitful peace. One that lulled you with its cool breeze and clear sky into a false comfort. For lurking in the shadows, waiting for you to close your eyes, were snakes, scorpions, and all manner of poisonous creatures. In that respect, the desert was a perfect spot for a town like Las Vegas. It's not that I didn't like the place—I certainly did. But I also recognized it for what it was—a den of vipers—and I for one, had no plans on getting snake bit. And yet, here I was, playing the snake charmer.

As I drove, my thoughts turned to Lizzie and her "entertainment," as she had called him. I wondered just what their arrangement was and what had caused sparks to fly between them. The parade of prostitutes certainly couldn't have helped. The trip to Vegas had likely turned sour and now Lizzie was at the man's mercy. A man she described as not being very nice was her ride back to California and she was stuck here, waiting it out. I felt a little sick to my stomach.

When I pulled into the porte-cochere of the Sands, Lizzie sat up in protest. "Oh, no. Not here, Maxie," she said. "Take me to your place."

"This is my place," I assured her. "I have a room here."

"You live here?" she asked. "You said you had a life."

"I do," I countered. "Right now that life is the Sands."

"Oh, Maxie, you're trying to trick me."

I assured her that was not the case as I pulled into my spot and worked on getting the top back in place. Lizzie waited. When the top was secure, I pulled my lid out of the trunk, rested it on my noggin, and brought Lizzie hers. She slipped out of the front seat and into my arms, reeking of gin.

"I've had a bit to drink," she said and laughed at her own cleverness.

I managed to get her upright and the hat on her head. She took my arm and held on tightly as we entered the casino.

"Take me to the bar," she said. "I need a drink."

"It would appear you've had enough of those," I offered. "How about I take you to your suite?"

She shook her head violently. "Gin and sin," she said. "I've had my gin, now I need my sin. Take me to your room."

"I don't think that's a good idea," I said.

"Well, I'm not going back with him." She tugged her arm from mine, almost falling with the force. I tried to grab her, but she pulled away. "If you won't take me, then I'll find someone who will."

Wasn't this lovely? Just the spot I was trying to avoid. A high roller's dame who wanted a new bedfellow. That was all I needed. "How about we get you some coffee?" I suggested.

"I don't want coffee," she said forcefully. She drew close again, playing the soft kitten. "Take me home, Maxie," she said. "I'll be a good girl. I promise."

I took hold of her and headed toward my room. What else was I to do?

"Was that man a friend of yours?" Lizzie asked as we made our way out to the garden area.

"What man?" I asked.

"The man at the El Rancho?"

"Keys?" I asked. "I already told you he was a friend."

"Not the musician," she said. "The other man. The one you were talking to when I came out of the ladies' room."

"Oh, him," I said. "A case of mistaken identity."

"On your part, or his?"

"Does it matter?" I asked.

"Not to me," she said, but I wasn't sure I believed her.

One of the stars Lizzie saw in the sky must have been lucky, because, with little effort, I got her to my room, managed to open the door, and took her inside. All without her falling.

Lizzie looked around the room. "Nice," she said. "Small."

"I prefer, cozy."

Lizzie giggled. "Wait here," she said. She headed for the bathroom, using the wall as a brace.

I removed my lid and placed it on the small desk, then I hung my suit jacket on the hook by the closet, and turned on the table lamp. Lizzie emerged minutes later clothed in nothing but her undergarments. She slid over to me and wrapped her arms around my neck. Then she kissed me. It was a soft kiss. A kind kiss. An inviting kiss.

She pulled back and smiled.

I put my hands on her hips. They were nice hips, soft and curvy, just like hips ought to be. They were inviting me as well. Inviting me to do things I had no business doing with someone I had no business being with. But there she was, standing in front of me, fiddling with my tie, wearing next to nothing, with perfect red lips, staring into my eyes. I pulled her head to my chest and she hugged me tightly.

Something came over me. A weakness to which I was all too prone. It came out before I even realized it. A promise I never should have made. "I can get you home," I said. Perhaps I was a soft sister after all.

"I don't want to go home," she said. "I like it here with you."

"I mean California," I said. "You don't have to rely

on Dorsey."

She looked up at me and smiled. "Aren't you sweet?" she said.

It isn't the word I would have used. I doubt it was the word Virginia would have used either.

We stood there holding each other for quite a time. Long enough that I felt Lizzie's body melt into mine. I took her in my arms, carried her over to the bed, and laid her down. She looked peaceful lying there, eyes closed, lost in slumber. I wondered if it was the only time she truly felt that way.

I went over to the chair, took a seat, and contemplated my ill-spent life, while I waited for time to pass. It would be another thirty minutes before Preston's shift would end, and probably another fifteen after that before he left. I noticed a lot in the back of the El Rancho and was willing to bet that was where employees parked.

The time passed like a tenth inning stretch at Fenway. But eventually, I donned my lid, pulled on my suit coat, and slipped out of the room, leaving Lizzie to her dreams, or possibly her nightmares. I took my Roadmaster from its dedicated spot and pointed it toward the El Rancho. When I arrived, I headed to the back of the property, got out, leaned against the driver's side door, and waited.

I was there about ten minutes when the first employees started coming out. Preston was not among them, but I hadn't expected him to be. There are things pit bosses need to do at the end of their shifts. Things that kept them there longer than the dealers.

I waited.

About fifteen minutes later a tall man came shuffling into the parking lot, head downward. He wore a brown, fitted Western-style suit with a wide, pinned collar and a lighter patch that formed a large V down his front. I wasn't sure, but it might have been designed by Nudie Cohn. I recognized him as the man I saw in the pit, so I approached.

"Preston?"

The man lifted his head. He looked weary. "Who's askin'?"

I extended my hand. "Name's Rossi. Max Rossi. I'm a friend of Frank Abbandandolo."

That caught his attention.

He took my hand and shook it. "What can I do for you, Mr. Rossi?"

"You can start by calling me Max."

"What can I do for you, Max?" he asked again.

I don't think he wanted to be there. I don't think he wanted me to be there either. It didn't stop me. "Mind if I ask you a few questions?"

He put his hand in his pocket and pulled out a deck of smokes. His stained fingers slipped one from the pack and tapped the end. He placed it between his lips, set it aflame, and sucked in a deep breath. He offered one to me. I declined.

"I suppose that depends on the questions," Preston said.

"I suppose it does at that," I agreed. "I heard your casino got hit the other night."

He raised an eyebrow, took another puff, then glanced around the lot. "Come with me," he said.

I followed him to his car, a Nash Metropolitan, white on the bottom and green on the top. It was a surprisingly small car for such a tall man. He had parked toward the back of the lot, more in the shadows. I didn't mind. Preston leaned against the front fender. "You askin' about something in particular?"

"I think you know the answer to that," I said, "but I'll bite. I'm asking about the Highwaymen in particular. I know they've hit your casino. Probably more than once. What can you tell me about them?"

"Damn little," Preston said. "We didn't even know they hit 'til we did the count. All I can tell you is these guys are good. Very good. And if we don't catch them, we're all going to be out of a job."

"So you don't know when they hit?"

"Not only don't we know when they hit, we don't even know how they hit or who they are. And we, of all people, should know."

"I don't follow you."

He took another deep puff.

"My brother-in-law's a Gaming Control agent," he said. "Gave us the inside scoop. But it didn't do any good. They still hit and we still missed them."

"Employees involved?" I asked.

"Probably," he said. "But who knows?"

"I was hoping you did."

Preston tossed his smoke to the ground. He moved to the driver's door and fished his keys from his pocket. "I'm sorry I can't be more help, Mr. Rossi," he said. "But I've told you everything I know."

We were back to Mr. Rossi.

"Is there any clue you can give me here at all?" I asked.

He opened the car door and moved to get in, then stopped. He reached into the pocket of his suit coat and pulled out a card. "Here," he said. "Go talk to my brother-in-law. Maybe you can make more out of it than I did."

I took the card and thanked him. He wished me luck, folded himself into his Nash, and headed out. I slid the card into my pocket and was about to head back to the Sands when I caught a sight out of the corner of my eye that stopped me in my tracks.

FIFTEEN

TWO MEN TALKING in the shadows at the back of the lot caught my attention. Partly because they seemed agitated and partly because I thought I recognized one of the voices. I stepped a little closer, being sure to stay in the shadows myself. When I got a better look, I recognized both of them. One was the guy who had almost scratched his arm off earlier in the evening and the other was Keys, still dressed in the same clothes he was wearing when we were with him, only this time he had on his jacket.

"This isn't going to work," the employee said. He was mixing dough with his hands. "They're going to find out and then where'll that leave me?"

Keys tried to reassure him. "They're not going to find out," he said. "Just play it smooth, the way we planned it. You're not alone in this."

"Easy for you to say. If we get caught, you'll just scoot away. Disappear into the darkness." He puffed his chest.

"Unless somebody shines a light on you."

Keys grabbed the man by his collar and yanked him close. "Listen here, Jasper," he said, his face mere inches from the man's own, "you do your part and no one will be the wiser. But if things go south and you start thinking of running your gums," he paused, "it won't go so well for you."

Even from this distance, I could see the man's saucer eyes.

Keys looked at him intently. "You gowed-up?" he asked?

"No, man. Not me!" the man protested.

Keys looked hard into his eyes. "You sure you're not using?" he asked.

"No, Keys," I swear. "I'm clean."

Keys let the man go, then straightened out his uniform for him. "Look, it's already working," he said in a much softer tone. "Just keep going the way we're going and it'll all be done before you know it. Now put an egg in your shoe and beat it."

The employee scuttled off. I moved into a shadow. Keys briefly scanned the parking lot, his eyes passing by me unnoticed, then headed to the hotel. I drove back to the Sands, wondering what I had just seen.

I put my car in its spot and went to my hotel room. It had already been a long night and I had the feeling it was about to get even longer. However, to my surprise, I found the room empty. Lizzie had vamoosed, along with her hat, gloves, purse, shoes, skirt, and enticing top. Perhaps there was some justice in the world after all.

I placed my suit coat and lid on their respective hooks, loosened my tie, and had a seat on the end of the bed. I liked the Sands; it was my place in the sun, but I was still a little apprehensive about the rooms. At least this one wasn't a suite. I pulled off my scarpe, tossed my tie onto the chair, then nestled my .38 under the pillow. I didn't think it would be needed, but why take chances?

I had a restless sleep that night. I spent part of it digging a hole out in the desert and the other part chasing Lizzie around the town, looking for a panther head bracelet. All the while, the envelope in the vent laughed at me. When I wasn't asleep, I was trying to piece together what I had seen in the El Rancho parking lot, wondering if I was closer to the Highwaymen than I realized. All I needed now was a raven to land outside my window and I'd be all set.

I wondered what I was going to do with Lizzie and how I was going to find the Highwaymen. But mostly I wondered why Fingers hadn't given me a room with a minibar. Maybe I should've offered to take Virginia to church tomorrow. Perhaps there was still time.

SIXTEEN

AFTER THE MORNING shower and shave, I gave Virginia a ring. It was Sunday, after all, and she was off, so I was hoping we might be able to make a morning of it—eggs, coffee, the works. Besides, I had a shiny new sax to show her. I let it ring several times, but there was no answer, so I retrieved the card Preston had given me last night from the inside pocket of my jacket and looked at the name: John Bentley Gaming Enforcement Agent. The chances of him being in his office on a Sunday were slim to none, but it didn't stop me from picking up the phone and giving the number to PBX.

After a couple of rings, a male voice came on the line. "This is John," the voice said.

"John Bentley?" I asked.

"Yes," he said. "Who am I speaking with?"

"Name's Rossi," I said. "I'm surprised to find you at work."

He chuckled. "I'm surprised myself," he admitted, "but I have a deposition tomorrow morning and I needed to do a bit of preparation. How can I help you, Mr. Rosey?"

"Rossi," I corrected. "I was wondering if you'd have some time to meet. I have a matter I'd like to discuss with you."

"Can you give me more details?" he asked.

"I could, but I'd prefer to do that in person. I hate to bother you on a Sunday, but it's time-sensitive."

"Sure it can't wait until Monday?" he asked. "I don't really want to be here any longer than I have to."

Bentley agreed to meet me in an hour at his downtown office if I promised to make it quick. I tried Virginia's number a second time with the same results, before donning my lid and heading for the casino to check on our whale. I looked in all the pits, but the man was nowhere to be found. It was becoming a day full of surprises. Virginia wasn't home, Bentley was in his office on a Sunday, and now the whale was MIA. I went over to the pit boss to inquire as to Dorsey's whereabouts and was told he hadn't been there all morning. In fact, no one had seen him since last night.

Perhaps he was a late sleeper. Or perhaps Lizzie's activities of the night before had caused another row. Who knew?

I didn't have time to find out. I had an appointment to keep, so I headed to Gaming Control downtown. The Gaming Control Board was under the jurisdiction of the Nevada Tax Commission. It was officially established to provide regulations for the licensing and operation of casinos and other gambling joints. Its main job, however, was to curtail the undesirable elements that came as a package deal with vices like gambling. I'm not sure they were doing such a bang-up job. What I did know was that they were as welcome as an egg in a meatball. I was taking a chance going there, but I couldn't see any other option.

I found Bentley sitting behind a gray metal desk in an office with his name painted on the door. It was an office with all the modern conveniences, phone, desk calendar, pen and pencil set. Even a business card holder. Clean enough to eat a meal off of; nothing like the police stations I'd seen. The walls were battleship gray. The furniture metal and of a matching hew. Awards, citations, and photos with important people spruced the place up a bit and gave me the feeling I was speaking to somebody important. I suppose that was the intent.

Bentley was a cordial man with a round face and a welcoming grin; the kind of man who made people feel immediately at ease. His desk was covered with folders, stacked on top of each other in neatly organized piles. A cigarette burned silently in his ashtray, the smoke curling upward.

"Have a seat," he said, pointing to the metal chair at the front of his desk. "How is it I can help you?"

I unbuttoned my jacket and took the seat, placing my lid on my lap. "I spoke to your brother-in-law last night," I began. "He told me you might know something about a group of cheaters, called Highwaymen, who've hit the El Rancho."

He folded his arms and leaned back in his chair. "Did he?" he asked.

"He did," I confirmed, wondering if it was the mention of the Highwaymen or his brother-in-law that had set him off.

"Who'd you say you worked for?"

"I didn't. Not just yet."

He gave me the once over. "You don't look like a

newshawk," he said. "No pad and pencil. I'd go more with a house dick, probably from a competing casino. Maybe one of the New York properties, if I'm judging your accent correctly. But just in case, anything I tell you is off the record."

"I can live with that," I said, adding, "and I hail from Bean Town, not the Apple."

"My mistake," Bentley said.

"Preston told me you filled him in, but it didn't stop them from hitting the El Rancho."

Bentley sat forward in his chair and placed his hands on his desk. "Preston's an idiot," he said. "I'll never understand why my sister married him. I told that lug what to watch for. Apparently, it didn't stick."

"So you know the Highwaymen are in town?"

He gave me a sly grin. "Of course we know. It's our job to know."

"Then why aren't they in bracelets?" I asked.

Bentley's grin faded. "Knowing they're here and knowing how to find them are two different things." He opened the top drawer of his desk. "Let me show you something," he said and removed a rack of chips. He laid them out in five stacks of five chips. They were all the same color red.

"Pick a stack," he said.

I pointed to the stack in the center. Bentley looked me straight in the eye and pushed it toward me.

"Notice anything different?" he asked.

I looked down at the chips, there were still five in the stack, but now the middle chip was green, while the others were still red.

"How'd you do that?" I asked.

"Pick another stack," he said.

I picked the one on the end, left side. Bentley slid the stack to me again, only this time I kept my eye on his hand. When he removed it, the second chip was now green, but I couldn't tell how it got there.

"You're pretty good at that," I said.

"No," he countered. "I'm a complete hack, but the Highwaymen are not. They're experts with the sleight of hand. If I can do this, imagine what they can do. Now, are you going to tell me why you're here?"

"You were right about the house dick," I admitted. "I work for the Sands. We're worried about getting hit."

"And well you should be," he said.

"I'd appreciate anything you could tell me."

"The El Rancho isn't the only casino they've hit," Bentley began. "They've been in town a couple of weeks now. There's usually a front man. Someone who goes in first and cases the joint; has a look around, scopes the place out. Sees what they're up against. What they have to worry about and what they don't. These aren't people who like surprises. After the front man reports back, they make a plan. They come in, hit hard, and leave quickly.

"The roulette table is one of their favorite marks. They work in pairs. After the dealer waves for no more bets, one of them will usually try to put a bet down, while the dealer is busy with that player, his partner will wait for the ball to drop and either increase his bet or change it."

"How do you spot the front man?" I asked.

"He could be anyone," Bentley said. "He just needs the time and ability to look around without sticking out too much."

"What about inside men?"

Bentley nodded. "There's usually employees involved. Dealers will pay off more than the bet by switching the chips with higher ones, like I did. Craps is good for that trick. Of course, they don't just play with chips. They do cards as well. The inside man will sneak out a deck from the hotel so the player can switch cards during the game."

"Wouldn't there be extra cards in the deck then?" I asked.

"They take care of that in the cut," he said. "The dealer will usually make some gesture that excuses his hand movement to slip a card in his pocket or he'll make sure the added card is at the top of the deck so the player can palm it when he cuts the deck."

"Anything I should look for?"

Bentley thought for a moment. "Things that look out of place," he said. "Maybe a fellow using the wrong hand or keeping his hand in a strange position. Something like that."

He pulled out a deck of cards and shuffled them. He pushed the deck to me. "Cut the deck and show me the bottom card."

I did as asked and produced a three of clubs. Bentley cut the deck and produced a five of diamonds.

"You shuffle them this time," he said. "Then cut again."

I did so, and this time produced a jack of spades. "I think I've got you," I said.

Bentley smiled and cut the deck. He produced an Ace. "Shall we bet next time?" he asked.

"You oughta take that act on the road," I said. I put my lid back in place and stood. "Thank you for your time," I said and extended my hand.

Bentley stood and shook it. "I don't suppose you'll clue me into anything you find?" he asked. "We've been looking to take them down for some time now. Even got close once."

"Oh?" I said.

"We'd actually identified the leader," Bentley said. "A fellow by the name of Walter Penn. From the Orleans area."

"What happened?" I asked.

Bentley raised an eyebrow. "Someone got to him first."

I heard the envelope laugh.

"You say you're from the Sands? That's Lansky's property, isn't it?"

"Is it?" I asked. "As far as I know, Jake Freedman owns the place."

"Sure, have it your way," Bentley said. "Only these Highwaymen aren't your typical thieves. There's a reason they've never been caught. We could put them away for good."

"I'm sure you could," I said. "But my job's to protect the Sands. Not run grifters out of town."

"And if your boss catches them? Then what? Or is that just not your problem?"

"Jack? Why he's just an old Texas oilman."

"It ain't Jack I'm worried about."

I let that lay. Then I tipped my hat and turned to leave.

"You go heeled?" Bentley asked.

"On occasion," I confirmed.

"Good, 'cause you're gonna need it," he said and took his seat.

I was about to leave a second time when an idea struck me. A hard slam out to left field, heading for the Green Monster. "What about a high roller?" I asked. "Could he be the front man?"

Bentley rubbed his chin for a moment. "Sure," he said. "I don't see why not."

SEVENTEEN

I DROVE BACK to the Sands, thinking about everything Bentley had just told me. If a high roller could be a front man, then I had a sneaking suspicion the Sands might be next on the Highwaymen's list. I thought about the time I spent on the tables with Dorsey. How he had held his hand strangely, cutting with his left, but sorting his chips with his right. How he wasn't really playing for sport, but seemed more interested in everything but the game. Of course, if he was a dealer at another casino, he wouldn't need to pay as much attention as a regular player. It'd be routine to him, doing it eight hours a day, five days a week.

When I got to the Sands, I headed straight for surveillance. I knocked on the door and was let in by Charlie.

"How's our whale?" I asked.

"Missing," Charlie said. "Hasn't been here all day."

"Anything come to you?" I asked.

He nodded. "I used to work in a bicycle club in New Orleans."

Bicycle clubs were joints that allowed cards, but no other form of gambling. Some were legit, most were not. If there's a vice, or a business which caters to a vice, you can bet the Mob's got their mitts in it up to the elbows.

"This guy was a dealer, only his name wasn't Dorsey," Charlie said.

"Wasn't Penn, was it?" I knew the answer, but I asked anyway.

"No," Charlie said. "It was Harris. Thomas Harris."

"And we don't know where he is?"

"Not a clue."

"You sure he wasn't cheating?" I asked.

"He wasn't cheating," Charlie said. I'd bet my life on it.

After what I saw today, I wasn't sure that was a safe bet.

I left surveillance and headed straight to the Whirlaway suite. I rang the bell several times but got no answer, so I went into the casino, hoping to run into Fingers, but came away with the same results. I suppose Fingers could have been with Dorsey, but somehow it didn't fit. I had missed breakfast and my stomach was telling me that missing lunch as well was not a good idea, so I headed for the Garden Room.

I ordered Chicken en Casserole, Mascotte and a manhatten or two to wash it down. If Dorsey was the Highwaymen's front man and he was no longer here at the Sands, it was likely he was meeting with them at this very minute, making a plan to hit the place. That could be tonight, tomorrow, or even right now.

The security officer's words came back to me. Sure,

Dorsey was seeing doxies, but the officer also said that single men were coming to the room as well. Now I wondered if instead of sex parties, were those people just part of the gang? Was he doing it right under our noses? Was the Whirlaway suite a meeting place for the Highwaymen? And if that were the case, what was Lizzie's involvement in this whole thing?

I ate my meal far too fast to enjoy it.

I needed to get to the casino, but I had something else to do first. Not hearing from Virginia was not sitting well with me and I wanted to make sure she was all right, so I headed to her apartment. When I arrived, I found her T-bird resting patiently in its spot, something I hoped was a good sign.

I rang the bell, and when no one answered, I knocked on the door but received the same. I put an ear against the door and thought I heard a noise, so I knocked again. "Virginia, it's Max," I said.

After a moment, the front door opened. Virginia stood in a housecoat she held closed with one hand. Before I could say a word, she slapped me so hard across the face that my lid fell to the ground. Then she slammed the door closed.

I reached down and picked up my lid, brushed it off, and looked for damage. It had fared better than my ego, so I slipped it back on my head where it belonged. I was about to knock again when a voice from behind spoke up.

"I don't think she wants to see you," it said.

I turned to find the supe, no better shaven than I'd found him before.

"Maybe you ought to just go," he said, forcefully. "She seems pretty mad."

There was an understatement.

I could feel my fist curling up. I wanted to hit

something or someone—probably this guy in front of me—but what good would that do? It wasn't him I was sore at; it was me, and punching myself in the kisser, somehow didn't seem appropriate. Where was Sal when you needed him?

I took the supe's advice and climbed back into my Roadmaster. I sat there for a moment. I knew what had happened. Nancy had called Virginia and reported the night's events. Except that report only took in one side of the story. There was another to tell, but this wasn't the time or the place, so I drove back to the Sands with my tail between my legs.

I spent the evening on the casino floor watching the tables, concentrating on craps and roulette, but watching the card games as well. I made a couple of bets on my own, just to blend in, but kept my eyes on the players. I'm not sure what I expected to find. If the Highwaymen were better at what they did than Bentley's pony show, there was no way I was going to spot them. Instead of hands, I watched eyes. I looked for people paying more attention to the dealer or their surroundings than to the game, their own cards, or their own chips.

It was a long night; one I was about to end when I saw Lizzie walk through the casino.

EIGHTEEN

LIZZIE WAS CLAD in a high collar blouse that tied around her waist and green striped capris, which accented her calves and hips nicely. She carried an oversized woven purse, her cheaters in the outside pocket. The look was good, but the luster had faded. She was ambling her way through the casino with no apparent destination.

When she saw me approach, she picked up her pace and looked away. "Don't talk to me," she said when I caught up to her. "I'm mad at you. I'm not a girl used to being turned down, you know."

"I'm not a man used to having my face slapped, but here we are," I said.

She stopped and turned to me, her ice-blue eyes demanding answers. "Where did you go? I was all alone when I woke. It was dark and cold."

"I had some business to attend to," I said. "Look, we need to talk."

"I don't know that we need to talk at all. You've made

your intentions crystal clear," Lizzie said and started to walk away.

I took her by the arm. "What game are you playing here?" I asked.

"Let me go," she said. "I'm sure I don't know what you're talking about."

"Where's Dorsey?" I demanded.

"How should I know? I'm not his keeper."

"If not you, then who?"

"Let me go! You're hurting me!"

I released her arm.

Lizzie turned her face away.

I stepped in closer and touched her gently. "Have you eaten?" I asked.

She shook her head.

I took her to the Garden Room and chose a booth near the back where we could talk in private. I ordered the Chateaubriand Bouquetiere for two with the Duchesse potatoes and a hearts of palm salad that we could split. Then added a manhattan and a gimlet, instructing the waitress to use half gin and half Rose's lime juice—the only way to make a proper gimlet. I didn't know if Lizzie was a gimlet gal, but I had seen plenty of women drink them and I knew she enjoyed gin. Maybe a tad too much.

I tried again. "Where's Dorsey?"

She shook her head. "I don't know," she said softly. "He wasn't in the suite when I returned last night and he wasn't at the tables either."

"Where did you spend the night?" I asked.

"In the streets, like a proper doxie," she said. "That's what I am after all, isn't it?"

I'd seen Lizzie perform several acts in the last couple days, but pity hadn't been one of them. It didn't suit her. "What's going on, Lizzie?" I asked. "I know you and Dorsey haven't been getting along. I know about the fights and the roundheels parading in and out of the room."

"Well aren't you the shamus?" She opened her purse and pulled out a pack of thin cigarettes and a book of matches. I took the book and lit the cigarette she had slipped in her mouth. She inhaled deeply, then blew the smoke over our heads. She held the thing between her fingers, her elbow on the table. "If you know so much, why don't you tell me what's going on?"

The waitress came with our drinks. Lizzie brought hers to her lips and took a delicate sip. I waited.

She took another puff. "He likes the ladies," she finally said. "He likes other things as well."

"What do you mean by other things?" I asked.

She checked to see if the words were floating in her drink.

"He kickin' the gong around?" I asked.

She nodded. "I think so."

I thought opium had gone out in the forties; apparently there were still some holdovers. But I had a feeling sucking on the mud pipe wasn't Dorsey's only perversion. "He having sex parties in the room?" I asked.

Her eyes widened. "I don't know," she said. "I always left when people came. I wanted no part of it all."

"Why did you two argue?"

"I'd had enough and wanted to go home. He'd won plenty at the tables. He could have paid for bus fare, but he refused. 'We're in this together,' he said. 'As long as I'm here, you're here.'"

"I told you I could get you home," I said.

"I know." She let her words trail off, then took another sip of courage. "But you abandoned me."

"It wasn't intentional," I said. "I told you, I have work to do around here. I'm not just a pretty face."

"I get it, I'm just an assignment."

"Let's not start that again," I said. "Regardless of the status of your current relationship, you're with the high roller who's playing at the very casino that signs my checks. I like those checks. I've grown very fond of them. They pay my rent and keep me in manhattans."

The waitress brought our food and we ate in silence, sharing both the meal and the sadness that had invaded Lizzie's life.

After a while, I spoke. "What are you going to do now?"

"Go back to the suite, I guess."

"I meant after that," I said.

"Why? You want to come over?"

I didn't answer. Lizzie pulled out another cigarette from the pack, lit it awkwardly, then inhaled. "I guess I'll find another man," she said and blew out the smoke. "How hard can that be in a town like this?"

"And you really don't know where Dorsey is?" I asked.

"No, and I don't want to know."

I gave her a minute to get comfortable with that answer. Her eyes gave nothing away, but her cigarette hand wasn't as sure of it. She took two more quick puffs. "Don't trust me?" she asked. "Would you like to see the suite?"

"I don't see how it would hurt," I said.

"Fine," she said with a huff and pressed the cigarette out in the ashtray on the table. "Shall we?"

Lizzie made a spectacle of her exit. I signed the ticket, left a tip, and followed her out to the garden area. She took her time sauntering along the path.

I stayed with her.

"Such a waste," she said.

"How's that?"

"Such a romantic place, and me without my Romeo."

"As I recall, it didn't work out so well for those two young'uns. Perhaps you're better off."

"Oh, Maxie," she said. "Can't you give a girl your arm?"

I gave her my arm. What would you do?

When we arrived at the suite, Lizzie pulled the key from her purse and handed it to me. I used it to open the door. She went in first and I followed. I was only two steps into the foyer when the sweat began to gather at the back of my neck. Lizzie laid her purse on the entrance table and slipped off her heels. She turned to me.

"Are you okay?" she asked.

"Right as the mail," I assured her. I placed my lid on the table and followed her into the main room.

There was a living space large enough to host a fancy lounge act, and enough empty bottles to have filled all their glasses. The room was framed on one wall by ceiling to floor curtains. Lizzie went over and flung the curtains open wide with two hands, revealing a large sliding glass window that led out into the pool area. It was a fine window, one that wasn't shattered into a thousand little pieces. One that didn't have a recently wedded bride on her honeymoon standing in front of it as a man threw lead at her.

I pulled out my handkerchief and wiped the back of my neck.

Lizzie turned to me. "You sure you're all right?"

"Just a little Déjà vu."

"Oh? You've been in this suite before?"

"Not this particular suite, but one like it." I could feel the sweat returning to my neck. "Anything left to drink?" I asked.

Lizzie moved to the bar. "I'm sure I can find something," she said. "Dorsey's room is over there if you want to see if he's hiding under the bed."

I went to his room while Lizzie found us something to drink. It looked like any other room, only larger. It smelled of whiskey and stale cigars. I opened his closet. There were three nice suit coats—blue, brown, and gray—several shirts, two pairs of shoes, and a collection of ties. Enough to keep a man happy. Two suitcases rested upright on the floor under the suits. I walked over to the bed. It was unmade. There were short glasses and two bottles of Old Fitzgerald: one empty and one still holding a small snort. Several cigar butts littered an ashtray that needed emptying.

Sticking out from underneath the ashtray was a card. I slid it out and had a look at it. The name was familiar, Vinny "Keys" Collins "Musician, Boozehound, Grifter." My prospects just got better. Too bad though, I was beginning to like the guy. I slipped the card into the inside pocket of my suit and headed for the bedroom door.

I stepped out of the room and into the hall. The door to the next room was slightly ajar, so I took it as an invitation to enter. Try and stop me. The odor from this room was much more pleasant. It was a familiar scent. The scent of a woman. I stepped inside. Everything in this room was in its place. The bed was made; a silk, see-through nightie rested across the end. Slippers on the floor. I went to the closet. There were dresses and sweaters and pants; many of which I recognized as purchases from one of our outings.

There were also two suitcases on the floor next to an

array of shoes. One was large and the other small, the size a child would use. I bent down to get a closer look. The suitcase looked old; its edges worn. The handle cracked. Underneath the handle, stamped in metal that had once likely been colored gold, were the letters "VP."

"See anything you like?"

I turned to find Lizzie, a drink in each hand, standing at the doorway.

"Just admiring your shoes," I said. "I have a bit of a fetish."

She handed me the drink. "Don't tell me you're one of those guys who goes around in women's heels."

"Oh, no!" I protested. "Nothing like that. It's more along the lines of what they do to a woman's legs. Defining the calf. Emphasizing the...well, you understand."

Lizzie smiled. "Perhaps if you had to walk in them, you wouldn't be so enamored."

She was probably right.

"Did you find him under the bed?" she asked and took a sip.

"All clear," I confirmed.

"Then you're satisfied he's not here?"

"Absolutely," I said.

Lizzie stepped closer to me and rubbed her hand on my chest. "Would you like to check my drawers just to make sure? I bet you could find something you'd like."

"I'm sure I'd find more than that," I said.

"I don't get you, Maxie. You offer to take me home. You're single. You have no problem kissing me, but you reject all my advances. Aren't you sweet on me?"

"I've already given you the lowdown. Nothing's changed."

Lizzie put her arms around my neck. "Then perhaps

you'd better leave," she said.

Her lips wanted me to kiss them, her eyes accomplices to the crime. She moved so close even the Holy Ghost couldn't have squeezed in between us. The nuns would not have approved.

I reached up behind my neck and took hold of her wrists, placing her arms down by her side. "I think it's best if we don't," I said and handed her my drink.

"One for the road?" she asked, doing little to hide her disappointment.

I shook my head. "Better not."

She followed me to the foyer. I placed my lid back in position, pulled open the door, and left quickly before she asked me again to stay.

NINETEEN

I SPENT ANOTHER restless night waiting for the sun to knock on my window. I got tired of waiting and decided to freshen up, hoping it would change my disposition. I had just pressed lather to whiskers when the phone rang in my hotel room.

I picked up the receiver and pressed it to my ear, "Yeah," I said.

"That you, Rossi?" the male voice asked. I recognized the Boston-Irish brogue. It belonged to a big, thick, ruddy-complexioned homicide detective named Queeney with whom I'd become acquainted.

"The one and only," I confirmed.

"You dressed?"

"Awful forward question. I hardly know you."

"Cut the wisecracks and get yourself over here to the El Rancho."

"The El Rancho?" I questioned. "What would make me want to go there?"

"How about a stiff with a room key to the Sands in his pocket?"

"I'll be right over," I said and hung up.

I spent the next few minutes trying not to slice my own throat, then pulled on my shirt, tie, suit coat, and the rest of the fixin's. I decided to leave the .38 in the drawer. I doubted the dead man would pose much of an immediate threat and bluebottles are apt to get nervy when there's a gat in your pocket.

I was at the El Rancho in less than twenty minutes. The sun had slept in this morning and was just making an appearance. I hadn't asked Queeney where the body was, but it seemed one of the bungalow rooms was the safe bet. As soon as I pulled around to the back, it wasn't hard to find the right spot. The police had made sure of that. They surrounded an end bungalow to the left side of a row. Probably a suite. I walked up to the two uniformed officers standing in front of the tape, introduced myself, and informed them I was expected. It didn't seem to have much of an impact. Luckily, Queeney poked his head out of the room and spotted me.

"Let that man pass," he barked.

I slipped under the tape and flashed the boys an appropriately smug grin, then made my way to the room. I was right; the place was a suite and an active one at that. There were bottles and glasses and more bottles tossed haphazardly about the main room. It resembled what I had seen in Dorsey's suite only on a grander scale. Ashtrays were full of cigarettes, some of them smokes, others reefers. Underwear was also strewn about. Bras hanging from lampshades. Panties on the couch and chairs. None of them occupied.

"The body's this way," Queeney said.

I went with him into the rear bedroom and there, lying on the bed, naked as the day the doctor spanked him, was Richard Dorsey, the Sands' whale, as dead as they come. He was lying on his back, looking up at the ceiling, his eyes wide, his arms down by his side, his legs spread. Even with his life force drained from his body, Dorsey was larger than he looked in his suit. Muscular enough to be a bouncer or a prizefighter, but with none of the scars. I wondered why he had chosen to be a dealer. The edges of Dorsey's back had that purplish-red discoloration that meant his blood had already pooled there. It also meant Dorsey'd been there a while. I'd seen it before, when people took their sweet time calling my father, allowing the red blood cells to sink and rigor mortis to set in. It only made it harder to dispose of the body.

"Know him?" Queeney asked.

I nodded.

"Good, then perhaps you can tell me why a guy who was high rolling at the El Rancho would have a room key to a suite at the Sands." Queeney held out the key. A plastic tag was attached to it and printed on one side were the words "The Sands" and "Whirlaway Suite."

Dorsey being a high roller at the El Rancho was news to me. "Was he registered to this room?" I asked.

Queeney shook his head. "He'd been registered here before though. Hadn't been here in a couple of days, according to management. With the key to a suite, I figure he got a better offer at the Sands."

"He's been a high roller at the Sands for several days now," I confirmed. "Went by the name of Dorsey, Richard Dorsey."

Queeney pulled his notepad from his shirt pocket and flipped through the pages. "Dorsey, huh? Looks like he went by Slater here, Clifton Slater."

"That's not even the best of it," I said. "His real name is likely Thomas Harris."

Queeney pinched his eyebrows. "You sure of that?" he asked.

"I wouldn't take it to the bank," I said. "But I wouldn't take odds against it either."

"How do you know?" Queeney asked. He took what passed for a pencil in his oversized mitt and began scratching in his notebook.

"One of the surveillance guys recognized him from a bicycle club in Orleans. The guy's good with faces. Said he was a dealer there."

"And you trust him?"

"Like I said, I wouldn't take odds against it."

"I'm gonna have to question him," Queeney said.

I nodded. "What happened here?" I asked.

"Maid found him this morning. Had a do not disturb on the knob for days. They finally decided to take a peek inside. Looks like a sex and hop party."

"Opium?" I asked.

Queeney nodded. "Probably. That and a little marihuana tossed in for fun. What I can't figure is why he done it here? Why not at the Sands?"

I thought I might know. "He brought a doll with him from California," I said. "She's staying in the suite. Looks like he might have tried the party there, but it didn't go over so well with her."

"She a Doxie?" he asked.

"Not in the true sense of the word," I said. "More of a companion."

"What's her name?"

"Elizabeth Averill."

"She still around?"

"As of last night," I said.

Queeney looked at me hard. "You involved in this, Max?"

"Not in this," I said, referring to the room. "But I was tasked with keeping Averill busy while the whale rolled on. We spent time together."

"Where were you Saturday night?" Queeney asked without looking at me.

"That when this happened?"

He looked up from his pad. "Just answer the question."

"I was with Lizzie at this very establishment," I said. "Watching the Dice Girls do their thing. One of the girls, Nancy, is a friend of a friend. You can ask her."

"Lizzie?" Queeney asked.

"Averill likes to be called Lizzie," I said.

"You with her all night?"

"Not the way you're implying, but yes, I was with her most of the night."

"How long is most?" Queeney asked.

"I had an errand to attend to," I said. "She was in my hotel room when I left, but gone when I returned. I assumed she went back to her suite."

"I think I've heard this song before," Queeney said. "It hasn't gotten any sweeter. How about you give me some times to play with?"

"I left around midnight and came back about an hour or so later, maybe longer."

Queeney continued scribbling. "Where'd you go?" he asked.

"Am I a suspect?"

Queeney stopped writing. He looked at me with hard eyes. "Should you be?" he asked.

"Look, Queeney, I've been straight with you, even gave you a hand up, told you more than you knew. But I can't go around telling Sands' business."

He pushed his lid forward. A hint of reddish locks peeked out from under. "You can try harder than that," he said.

I mulled over my options. Not that there was much to mull. Then I told Queeney about the Highwaymen and how they'd hit the El Rancho and were likely headed to the Sands. I told him I tried to get some information from some of the employees at the El Rancho, waiting until they got off the late shift. I explained I had some luck with one of the pit bosses who led me to Bentley at Gaming Control. I was careful to leave out Fingers, his goomah, and Keys. I also said nothing about my meeting with Lansky or being tasked with sniffing out the head.

"And you think this Dorsey guy was with the Highwaymen?"

"I think he may have been their front man," I said.

"But you didn't see him that night?"

"I didn't. But I didn't go into the casino or anywhere near the rooms," I said. "I hung out in the parking area until the employees showed. After that, I drove back to the Sands."

I'm not sure Queeney bought it, but it was all I had to sell.

"Why are you here?" I asked him. "I thought you worked homicide."

"What makes you think I don't?" he asked. "Murder or an overdose, that's up to the M.E. to decide. Until he does, it's a murder in my book."

"You got a suspect?" I asked.

"I was hoping it was you," he said with a grin.

I returned a wry smile.

"I got bupkis," Queeney said. "You find anything out, you call me."

"That only go one way?" I asked.

"It doesn't have to," he said.

"We done here?"

Queeney nodded.

I started for the door, then stopped. "I'll let you know what I find out," I said and left the room.

TWENTY

I DROVE BACK to the Sands, eager to tell Fingers what I had turned up. I put the car in its spot and scooted up to the mezzanine. As I was coming up the stairs, I met another coming down. I knew the man, his name was Salvatore Manella, though I almost didn't recognize him without his two shadows. Sal was a made guy from New York. A free agent, so to speak. Sure, he took orders, but he also mostly did as he pleased. He was dressed, as usual, to the nines, wearing a navy blue broadcloth sack suit, narrow in the shoulders and loose at the waist. His shirt was light blue and his tie paisley, perfectly matching his square. He fiddled with his monogrammed cuffs as he descended.

"Well, if it isn't Max Rossi," he said. "Fingers' bloodhound."

"Aren't you a couple of goons short?" I asked.

He pretended to laugh. "Aren't you on the wrong side?" he countered. "Your father must be so proud."

"At least I know who my father is without a blood test." I didn't wait for Sal to answer, I'm sure it wouldn't have gone well anyway. Instead, I continued up the stairs and headed into Fingers' office, where I found Leona standing guard.

"He in?" I asked.

"Maybe, she said. "Who's askin'?"

"Mr. Potato Head."

"Clever," she said. "Take a seat and I'll see if he wants to see you."

"Tell him I found Dorsey," I said. "And that it's urgent."

"How urgent?"

"Life or death," I said, then added, "Mostly death."

She gave me a curious look, then picked up the phone. Two minutes later I was sitting in the same chair at the same table with the same manhattan and the same cigar resting in the same ashtray. Only this time Lansky was missing.

"Whatcha got?" Fingers asked.

"I found Dorsey," I said. "In a hotel room at the El Rancho, getting measured for a wooden kimono."

Fingers raised an eyebrow, then began rubbing his chin. "This isn't good," he said.

"It's worse than you think," I continued. "Dorsey's not his real name. Charlie recognized him from a bicycle club in Orleans. Called himself Harris then. Called himself Slater at the El Rancho. Plus, I'm pretty sure he's the front man for the Highwaymen. Your connection led me to a Gaming Control agent who passed along the dope."

"You spoke to Gaming Control?" he asked and rubbed his thick hands together.

"I didn't have much of a choice," I said. "I wasn't getting anywhere. But don't worry, I didn't let on to the connection. Besides, it wasn't an even exchange. He told me what he knew and I acted the stooge, though it wasn't much of an act."

"What'd you learn?"

"A front man comes in and studies the operation. Sees what they're up against, the whole nine yards. Then they make a plan and hit. Dorsey was a high roller at the El Rancho before they hit there, then he moved here. May have been at other places too."

I went on to tell him about the time I played cards with the man, how he looked around at everything but the game. "Studying the employees, casing the joint, getting the lowdown on the place. I think a dealer's involved."

"How's that?" Fingers asked.

"Dorsey complained about not having his regular dealer right after getting the card he needed to turn his gutshot into a legitimate straight. Wouldn't play anymore until his dealer came to the table. I noticed at the time that he positioned his hand strangely, but didn't think anything of it. I think Dorsey had a pack of Bees on him and slipped the card in to finish the straight. Then he needed the dealer to help him get the fake out and the good card back in."

"How could he do that?"

"The dealer coughed real loud, caught everyone's attention. Dorsey must have given him a signal of some kind at that moment; told him what card to look for. The dealer had Dorsey cut the cards right after that. From what Bentley showed me, it wouldn't have been too hard to do."

"Bentley?" Fingers asked.

"The Gaming Control agent. He showed me some sleight of hand tricks that would have put the Great Cardini to shame. These Highwaymen are good, very good."

"So what happened to Dorsey, or whatever his name is?"

"Looks like an overdose. Could be accidental. Could be intentional. Looks like he was into the skirts, you know, ones that play around plenty."

"What about his girl? The one you been traipsing all over town with. She involved in any of this?"

I took a sip of the manhattan. It was early and it burned a little going down. It was a question I hadn't expected or maybe didn't want to expect. "I suppose she could be," I said. "But it doesn't look that way on the surface."

"Now what?" Fingers asked.

"I'd say we're next in line, but Dorsey's death doesn't sit well with me. If they were about to hit us, why'd they take him out? If they did take him out."

"And if they didn't?"

"Would you hit another casino with all eyes on you?" I asked. "Of course, there's nothing to say they know we've figured out who their front man is. Assuming we have. If it were me, I might just hit one more time before I skedaddled. Take the money and run."

I took another drink. Fingers took a puff. We shared some silence.

"I don't suppose you got the name of that dealer?" Fingers asked.

"Hollis, according to his name tag," I said.

Fingers picked up the phone. "Leona, connect me to the pit. Any pit."

Fingers waited, after a moment he began speaking.

"You got a dealer by the name of Hollis?" he asked. Whoever was on the other end of the line was giving Fingers news he didn't want to hear. I could see it in his face. That couldn't be good.

He put down the receiver. "He's smoke," he said. "Didn't show up for his shift last night. Didn't call in."

"I'd say that clinches it."

Fingers nodded. "Got any ideas?"

"I might," I said. "It's too late for undercover, but we might be able to stop them from hitting the place. Mind if I try them out?"

"Be my guest."

I downed the rest of my drink, then headed over to surveillance. I brought Charlie up to speed on everything, including Dorsey, letting him know as much as I did about their tactics and tricks. Everything I'd learned from Bentley.

"You think they'll hit tonight?" Charlie asked.

"It'll be busier at night and I'm guessing they'll want that cover. I've got some things to do, but I'll try to get back as soon as I can. When I do, I'll stay on the casino floor. See what I can see."

Charlie nodded. "I'll stay the night," he said.

"You don't have to do that. Just be sure to pass on the information."

"No, Charlie said. "It was my miss, my responsibility."

"Okay," I said. "Have it your way. By the way, there might be a detective looking to ask you questions about Dorsey. Big Irish guy. You can trust him."

I left Charlie and went to my room. I opened the dresser drawer and pulled out my .38, something told me it might come in handy. I took off my suit coat, put on my shoulder holster, and slid the gun in place. A gentleman would have gone and checked on Lizzie, but if I'd proven anything in the last couple of days, it was that I was no gentleman.

I was halfway to the front door when my conscience got the better of me. I turned and headed to the Whirlaway suite. When I got there, the door was open, and a bluebottle was standing with security. I peeked inside and saw Lizzie sitting on the couch, Queeney hovering above her. She turned and saw me.

"Oh, Maxie!" she called out.

Queeney came over and brought me in. "Can you give us a few minutes?" I asked.

"A few," he said, and let me go in by myself.

I sat down next to Lizzie. She turned and threw her arms around me. "Oh, Maxie," she said again. "Isn't it just terrible?"

I assured her it was.

She pulled back and looked at me. Her makeup running. "What am I going to do?" she asked.

"I told you, I can get you home."

She nodded and hugged me again.

"Lizzie," I said. "I need to ask you a couple of questions. They may not be questions you like."

She sat upright and nodded.

"Did you know Dorsey was cheating at the tables?"

Her eyes got big and she shook her head. "Of course not," she said. "I tried not to sit with him while he gambled and he never said anything to me about the tables. Do you really think he was?"

I didn't answer. "Do you know where he got the drugs from?"

She shook her head. "I never stayed in the room when he started doing that. I'd walk around the pool area or sit in the lounge. I didn't want to get involved."

I channeled my father and gave her stern eyes.

"He did try to get me to do it once," she admitted. "But I wouldn't. I think that's why he started bringing in those girls."

"Have you been with him the whole time he was in Las Vegas?"

"Yes, I told you I came up here with him."

"And you've been at the Sands the entire time?"

"Of course," she said and pulled back. "What are you asking, Max?"

I took her hands in mine. "Nothing," I assured her. "Don't fret over it."

Queeney stepped into the room.

"I have to go," I said to Lizzie.

She squeezed my hand. "Can't you stay?" she asked. "I don't want to be alone."

"I'll try to come back when I can," I said and left her in Queeney's care.

As I walked down the hallway, I knew one thing for sure. Lizzie was lying to me, not just about where she was with Dorsey, but about other things as well. I needed to know why and I needed to know it fast, so I headed to the El Rancho. It'd be too early to catch the dealer I saw the other night, but there was another person I needed to find first.

TWENTY-ONE

WHEN I ARRIVED at the El Rancho, I pulled around the back and went to the room number he'd written on the back of his card. When I got there, the room was being cleaned. I asked the maid if she knew where I could find the occupant and was told the room was scheduled for check out. I went inside to the front desk and asked if Vinny Collins had indeed checked out, but was told there was no one registered under that name. Vincent and Keys produced the same results. It shouldn't surprise me; Keys did talk about OPM. I don't know why I would expect that to be different with hotel rooms.

I needed to find Keys before the police did. I wasn't entirely sold on Queeney's promise to share and share alike. Those types of promises, like rivers, have a habit of flowing one way—especially once they had their man in bracelets. If I didn't get to Keys first, who knows what I'd actually find out. I was raised to trust the police about as far as they could be tossed, and Queeney wasn't a man easily thrown. I had about as much chance getting anything out of Keys once he was behind bars as I had with Joi Lansing, though I was still holding out hope on that front.

I did, however, have some other options.

As I headed back to my car, I saw Nancy Williams. She was dressed in shorts, hose, a button top with a high collar, and the type of flats dancers wore. I had seen Virginia dress the same way when she was rehearsing. Nancy was heading in the direction of the Round up Room with other girls I recognized from the stage.

"Nancy," I called out.

Nancy stopped when she saw me and motioned for the others to go ahead. She crossed her arms and positioned herself on one hip. "How's the cheek?" she asked.

News traveled fast in Las Vegas.

"You know, you oughta mind your own business," I said. "For your information, I wasn't on a date with that woman. She was the moll of a high roller I was tasked with. Besides, Virginia knew where I was. I told her I had to take the lady out."

"Does Virginia know she hung all over you?"

"I'm guessing she does now," I said.

Nancy stood straight. "You bet she does," she said, making sure to emphasize each word on my chest with her pointer.

"That was not by my choice," I said.

She crossed her arms again. "Well, you didn't exactly push her away."

"Actually, I did exactly push her away; something you didn't see. But she had a mind of her own, and it's a delicate situation when she's the king's queen. You should know that, you're in the game. Besides, it's not like Virginia's my steady girl."

"Does Virginia know that?" Nancy asked and walked away, leaving me standing there with no one to hold my jaw in place.

It was a good question. One I hadn't thought of before. What was I to say? Nancy was right, of course. But I didn't want her to be right. I wanted to be right. I wanted my actions to be justifiable, but they weren't. They were all wrong. I had managed to put myself in an impossible situation, all because I let my emotions get the better of me. Even if Virginia wasn't my steady gal, that didn't give me the right to act like a smitten schoolboy when offered the lips of another. I deserved the slap in the face—both of them.

I walked to my car. My head swinging low as if I'd been sent to the gallows. I flipped the attendant a dime and pointed the beast in the direction of Garwood Van's, hoping he might have a clue as to where to find Keys.

Garwood recognized me straight off when I entered. "It's the Selmer man," he said. "How's that new sax?"

"Haven't really had much time to test it out," I admitted.

"Too bad. You've got some chops, my man."

I told him I appreciated that and then asked if he'd seen Keys lately.

"Not since he came in with you," he said. Then grinned, "That boy's harder to hold on to than a greased pig. Let me guess; he owes you money."

"Something like that," I said.

Garwood turned his head slightly and studied me. "You're not hitting the pipe, are you? That why you're lookin' for him, son?"

So Garwood knew about Keys after all. Knew, but apparently allowed it to happen. "Not me," I assured him. "I don't even smoke." I crossed my heart with my forefinger. "I'm strictly a manhattan man."

"Good," he said. "Too many musicians are hopheads. It ain't good for you. Now mind you, a little juju once in a while never hurt anyone, but that hard stuff'll kill ya."

I decided to take a shot. "Is Keys selling more than marihuana?" I asked.

Garwood turned and shuffled some music in a bin. It didn't look like it needed to be shuffled, but what did I know? I waited.

"Keys is an interesting fellow," Garwood finally said. He turned to me. "Plays the ivories like nobody's business. He's better'n anybody I know, myself included. Got the kind of talent that can really take a man places," he said with a smile. "The good Lord sure blessed that man's fingers."

He paused a moment and his face changed. A sadness swept over him as he continued. "But the devil put a demon inside him, just to even the score. And a mean one at that. The kind that rips at your soul and tears it into tiny little pieces. So small you can't put them back together. The kind of demon that spreads to other people and tears at them as well. Keys is a fellow best to keep at arm's length, if you know what I mean."

I knew what he meant.

"He won't stay here long," Garwood said. "He'll get himself in trouble—get those around him in trouble too—then he'll blow, leaving everyone else to clean up his mess. Course he'll come back, eventually. He'll wait just long enough for you to forget why he left in the first place. He'll come back, playing that sweet music and you'll wonder why he ever left."

Garwood was no longer looking at me. He wasn't even in the store any longer. A memory had stolen him away. I hoped it was a pleasant one.

"I don't suppose you know where I could find him?" I asked.

"He in trouble?"

"I don't know yet," I admitted.

"He's probably practicing with Jimmy Five over at the Bootlegger. They got a show coming up. Want me to tell him you're looking for him if he comes in?"

"Sure," I said and thanked him.

"Get on that sax," Garwood yelled out as I left.

I drove down to The Bootlegger, parked in the rear, and came in through the only door that was unlocked. I was immediately greeted with the aroma of marinara—sweet basil, oregano, Roma tomatoes—the food of the gods. I wasn't sure if they had those ingredients in heaven, but I knew I didn't want to go if they didn't. I had come in the kitchen and it was right about then that I realized I hadn't yet eaten.

The Bootlegger was paradise for an Italian: chicken parmigiana, pasta e fagioli, linguine alle vongole, risi e bisi, ragu all salsiccia, gnocchi, lasagna, and, of course, meatballs. I was a sucker for a good meatball.

"Oh, che ci fai qui?" a fat cook yelled out.

"Just passing through," I assured him.

He waved his hand at me, motioning me to come to him. "Vieni qui," he said.

"I'm just going to the showroom," I said. "Looking for Jimmy Five."

"Vieni, vieni qui," he repeated and waved like he was trying to put out a fire.

I went over to him.

"I hava somea tinga fora youa to... come si dice? "Ah, trya," he said, doing his best with the language. It was significantly better than my Italian.

He picked up a small white plate and brought it over to the stove, then he lifted the lid off a large pot. The

149

aroma of marinara slapped my face, then grabbed my nose and dragged me toward it. He dipped a large spoon into the sauce, pulled out two beautifully round meatballs, and laid them on the plate.

"You lika di polpetti?" he asked.

"Do I?" I said. "All I need now is a fork."

The fat cook handed me the plate and a fork. "I trya newa recipe," he said. "You lika?"

I cut into the meatball with the side of my fork. It was soft and juicy, the product of having sat in the sauce for hours. It brought back memories of my nonna, the one who was half Gypsy. Sunday mornings she would make meatballs in gravy and pour it over homemade pasta. Then the family would eat until my grandfather had to unbutton his trousers. Pasta shock we used to call it.

I slipped the meatball into my mouth and let it get acquainted. I barely had to chew the thing before it melted into beef, pork, and veal nirvana. The nuns had warned us many times of the impending second coming. If it had happened right then and there, I would have been ready.

"È buono? Ti piace?"

"Oh yeah," I said. "Mi piace very much!"

"Molto bene!" the cook said and slapped me on the back. I about fell into the sauce.

"Di," he said. "Bringa ita wita you," he said.

I thanked him and took the meatballs with me into the showroom. When I got there, Jimmy Five and the Dimes were all on stage, playing *Straight, No Chaser*. Keys was not with them. I took a seat and listened. Meatballs and Jazz. I really was ready for the world to end.

When the song concluded, Jimmy turned and found

me in my seat. "Well, hey, it's the sax man. Come to sit in?"

"Not today," I said with a mouth full of meatball.

Jimmy turned to the guys. "Let's take five," he said, then came and sat at my table. "If you're not here for the music, then why are you here?"

I pointed to what was left of the meatball.

Jimmy laughed. "That's Matteo," he said. "You can't walk through his kitchen without him giving you food. You learn to take a different door."

"I'm not sure I could do that," I said.

"You will if you still want to fit into your suit." Jimmy let me finish, then asked. "So, why are you here?"

"Looking for Keys," I said.

"Aren't we all," Jimmy countered. "He was supposed to be here; we got a gig this week. But he didn't show. Keys is a talented musician, but ain't one bit reliable."

"So I've heard," I said. I wiped my mouth and took a shot in the dark. "What do you really know about Keys?"

Jimmy looked at me suspiciously. "He in some sort of trouble?"

"Not yet," I said. "But maybe."

"This have to do with what you do at the Sands?"

"It could," I said.

"The Sands, that's Lansky's place, right?"

That was the second time I had been asked that same question, and I knew what both men meant. "Look, I'm not in the game, if that's what you're asking. I tried the life once, but it wasn't for me. I'm not looking to put a hurt on Keys. I just need to find out what he's up to and how deep he's in. I know he's selling drugs, but I don't know what else he's into."

"You on the up and up?" Jimmy asked cautiously.

I assured him I was, though it was mostly a lie. If Keys was running the Highwaymen, I sure didn't want him to know I knew it and I didn't know how close Keys was to Jimmy or what Jimmy would say to him. If he wasn't the leader, then so be it. I still needed to know what happened in that suite, and I had a feeling Keys could tell me.

"I know he sells reefer, but that's about it. He never really stays in one place for very long," Jimmy said. "Too bad, 'cause he's got the gift. Fact is, Keys ain't dependable and when you're trying to get yourself off the ground, dependability is one thing you can't do without. Sure, I let Keys sit in with us, but I'd never hire him full-time. It just ain't worth it."

I nodded.

Jimmy stood. "But you and your sax are welcome anytime," he said and extended his hand.

I took it.

"Sorry, I can't help you," he said.

"So am I."

"What are you doing Friday night?" he asked.

"Nothing I know of."

"Why don't you come with us? There's a kid, plays the sax, supposed to be pretty darn good. A bunch of us are headed over there. I'll hold a couple of spots for you."

"Where?" I asked.

"The Moulin Rouge, over on West Bonanza. Can't miss it."

"I'll see what I can do," I said. "No promises."

TWENTY-TWO

INSTEAD OF HEADING to the Sands, I went home. I had a couple of phone calls to make and I didn't want to make either of them at the hotel. The envelope greeted me as I walked in. I ignored it, threw my lid on the end table, and hung my suit coat over the back of the chair. My first call was to John Bentley, Gaming Control agent. I was hoping he'd be finished with his deposition by now and would be available for a little chitchat. My hope blossomed when he picked up the phone.

"This is John," he said.

"This is Rossi, we spoke yesterday in your office."

"Yes, I remember you. What can I do for you, Mr. Rossi?"

"My high roller is dead," I said.

"Oh?"

"I'm pretty sure he was the front man for the Highwaymen. He was playing the same role at the El Rancho under a different name."

"How did you discover that?"

"The police called me when his body was found there, a Sands room key in his pocket."

"Murdered?"

"That or an overdose, the jury's still out."

"Let me see what I can find out. You free later this afternoon?"

I told him I was and then asked for a favor. "Could you run a name for me?"

"You think it's connected?"

"I'm certainly beginning to," I said. "The name's Vinny Collins, though his given name could be Vincent. Also goes by Keys. He's a musician out of California by way of Orleans."

"Drop by later this afternoon. I'll see what I can do." Bentley paused, then added: "And thank you."

My next call was to my father. I spent the first part of it appeasing my mother, assuring her I'd visit soon and was making sure I was eating from the three food groups: pasta, rice, and pasta. Then I waited as she called my father to the phone, giving me one last guilt trip before she handed it off to him.

"You find who you were looking for?" my father asked.

"I think I'm close," I said. "I was wondering if you'd ever heard of Walter Penn, a grifter from the Orleans area?"

The phone stayed silent as my father ran the name around in his head. I'd seen him do it before and I'd learned over the years it was best to wait and let him pull up whatever there was to recall.

"I hearda him," he finally said. "A Spanish grifter. Went by the name Pirata Penn. Got caught up with some boys out in California. It didn't end well for him.

Why are you asking?"

"He might have been the big pillow at one time."

"Interesting," my father said. "I'd always wondered what it was."

"Is that all you know about him?"

"Rumor is he married a voodoo princess and the two had a daughter, but I don't know if any of that's true. It wasn't anything I was involved in."

One of the reasons my father was so respected, one of the reasons even opposing families used him, was because he didn't stick his nose where it didn't belong. He didn't ask questions about things he didn't need to know. It wasn't a lesson his offspring learned very well.

"I think someone might've cast a line and caught a whale," I said.

"Catch and release?" my father asked.

"No," I said. "Not able to release this one. Past its expiration date."

"Were they intentionally fishing for whale?"

"I don't know for sure, but my gut's telling me the bait was intentional."

He admonished me to be careful. I assured him I would and hung up the phone. I looked up at the envelope. I could tell it was grinning at me and I would have slapped the grin off its smart mug—if it had one. Instead, I returned my hat and suit coat and headed back to the Sands.

After I put the car where it belonged, I went straight to the Copa Room. I probably shouldn't have, but I needed to square things with Virginia. Nancy's words were eating at me like week-old eggplant parmigiana. As I hoped, the girls were on stage, practicing. I took a seat at one of the tables and waited.

When Virginia caught sight of me, her face went sour. That wasn't a good sign. Fifteen minutes passed before they took a break. Virginia flashed me a purposeful glare, then spun on her heels and went backstage. I stood and walked to the front of the room. The man in the black slacks and turtleneck shook his head and walked away.

I was about to jump up on stage when Cat greeted me. "I don't think she wants to speak to you," she said.

I tried a humble look. "She tell you everything? Send you out here?"

"Me? No, a girl can just tell when things aren't right. You cheat on her?"

"Not in so many words," I said.

Cat looked at me skeptically. "Women are like wild horses," she said.

There was one I hadn't heard before. "Really?" I asked. "How do you figure?"

"You can't just walk up and put a bridle on them," she said. "You've got to pamper them a bit. Coddle them. Earn their trust. Wild horses don't trust easily, you know. Especially when that trust has been lost." She paused. "You can't just jump back in. She's going to need some time."

"And what am I to do? Wallow in my misery?"

"Did you create that misery, or did she?"

It was a good point. I didn't like good points, especially when they went against me. "How do you know so much about horses?" I asked.

"I'm not going to be a Copa Girl forever," she said. "I plan to own a horse ranch one day."

"Here in the desert?" I asked.

"Sure, why not? Horses live all around here wild, you know. Haven't you ever heard of mustangs?"

"One mustang," I admitted. "Fellow by the name of Desert Dust. Hailed from Wyoming. Made a motion picture about him in Hollywood. Saw it in the theaters. Trigger, Silver, and Desert Dust is all I know about horses."

Cat smiled. "Give her time," She said.

I nodded and turned to leave. As I made my way toward the door, I understood something my father had once tried to teach me many moons ago. It was amazing how important something became once you couldn't have it anymore.

TWENTY-THREE

I HEADED TO my meeting with Bentley at Gaming Control. It was the second time my tail was fixed firmly between my legs. Luckily, Bentley didn't seem to notice. He looked much the same as he had when I saw him before, only this time the cigarette was hanging from his lips and his desk had more folders.

He motioned for me to take a seat. "What's going on?" he asked. The cigarette bounced up and down as he spoke.

I told him about Dorsey, including all the aliases he used and his connection to the bicycle club in New Orleans. I included Dorsey's stint as a high roller at both the Sands and the El Rancho and indicated that he was probably connected to the other casino that was hit as well.

"And this Vincent 'Keys' Collins? What's his part in all this?" Bentley asked.

"That has yet to be determined," I said.

Bentley removed the cigarette from his mouth and took his time putting it in the ashtray. He looked at me the way cops do. "But you wouldn't have asked me to run him if you didn't suspect him of something."

"Fair enough," I said. "But just in case, you tell me what you found first and then, if it fits, I'll tell you what I know."

Bentley picked a folder from the top of a pile and opened it. "Vincent Beaumont Collins, musician, a.k.a. Keys, was born in New Orleans, Louisiana. His mother was a Creole native named Dolliole and his father was a Spanish import named Allegre Santiago, who changed his name to Collins when he came ashore." He looked up at me. "Guess he wanted to fit in."

"That all?"

"Your friend's a busy boy. Got arrests up and down the coast and is currently wanted in both Louisiana and California."

"Let me guess. Possession with intent to sell."

Bentley tapped his nose. "Now, what's the connection?"

"It looks like Keys supplied the drugs that sent Dorsey over the edge." I pulled the card from my inside pocket and handed it to Bentley. "I found this on the nightstand in Dorsey's suite."

Bentley took the card and gave it the once over. "You think it was intentional?"

"That's the two-thousand-dollar question, isn't it? I knew he was selling marihuana cigarettes, but I wasn't sure about anything else."

Bentley studied the folder. "Looks like opium as well."

That sat like lead in my stomach.

"You make him for the leader of the Highwaymen?"

"I think he's connected somehow. Any more than that would be pure speculation. Though I can't see why he'd want to bump off his own front man. Plus, it looks like there were parties at the Sands as well. If you were gonna do it, why not do it there?"

"I checked with the police, got a lieutenant," he looked at the folder, "McQueeney. Said the M.E. hadn't filed his report yet. You got a lead on this Keys?"

I shook my head. "Looked for him most of the morning. Came up with nothing. He's most likely skipped town."

"Unless he is connected to the Highwaymen."

It was a good point. But I had other things I needed to know. "What can you tell me about Pirata Penn?" I asked.

Bentley smiled and pulled his cigarette from the ashtray, decided it was too short, then got a fresh one and lit it. He offered one to me. I passed. "You've been doing your homework," he said.

"I was taught well."

Bentley took another folder from the stack. "I thought you might ask, so I pulled the folder. "Walter Penn, a.k.a. Pirata Penn, was born Gutierre Reyes Diaz Peña. Like Santiago, he anglicized his name as soon as he hit the Gulf."

"New Orleans as well?"

Bentley nodded. Married a woman by the name of Isadora, who claimed to be a voodoo princess."

"Was she?"

Bentley shook his head. "Highly unlikely, she wasn't the right race for it. Not that you have to be of African descent, but most of them are. Near as we can tell, Isadora was just a grifter, much like her old man. A palm reader who mixed curses for a price. I think Walter helped the curses come true. You know, to boost sales. Spanish origin, just like Walter, only her family had been in the states for quite some time by then. She was a looker," he said and handed me a photograph. "Had that exotic flair. Used it to her benefit."

I studied the photograph. There was a strange familiarity to it. Something around the eyes. It was always the eyes.

"I've done my homework, as well," Bentley said. "Massimo 'Max' Rossi, son of Boston Rossi with ties to the Boston mafia. Working for a casino run by the New York crime syndicate."

"Queeney tell you anything else?" I asked. "Did he tell you I don't have skin in the game?"

"For someone who claims not to be in the game, you sure do hang with the players."

I tossed the photo onto his desk. "We done here?" I asked.

"Don't get steamed," he said. "I just want to know which side you're on."

"How many mobsters come sit in your office?" I asked. "Bend your ear? Or is your hand out under the desk as well?"

Bentley's face hardened.

"What's wrong?" I asked. "Don't like the questions? Or is it the answers that've got you bothered?"

"Now see here," Bentley said.

I stood. "Before you go accusing someone of things you know nothing about, you'd better make sure the shoe isn't right at home on your own foot."

"Look, let's try this again," Bentley said in a calmer tone. "Please, sit down. I'm not lookin' to make enemies here."

I returned to my seat. Perhaps I was a little jumpier than I ought to have been. "Anything else about Penn in that folder of yours?"

"Looks like his wife died during childbirth. Gave him a daughter he named Veronica."

"You got a photo?"

Bentley shook his head. "Her father was careful not to take photos of her. At least not any that made it out into the public. She didn't even attend his funeral."

"That you know of," I said.

He didn't answer.

"Why'd he get taken out?" I asked, careful not to mention I knew anything about California's part in it.

"He was a grifter and the head of the Highwaymen. They hit gambling joints and bicycle clubs all over the country. I'm sure there were thousands of reasons anyone would want him dead."

"They find a body?"

"Oh yeah. You take out someone like that, you want people to know it."

I couldn't help but wish I had a photo I could send to my father. One look and he'd be able to tell me exactly who did the deed. Not that it mattered, I was just curious is all.

"I think they're going to hit the Sands," I said. "The way I see it, the death is going to shine a light, if not on them, then near enough. It doesn't really matter if they killed their front man or not, I figure they'll hit one more time then get while the gettin's good."

"They're awful careful," Bentley said. "They may be gone already."

"You're probably right," I admitted. I stood and replaced my lid. "I guess we'll find out in the next couple of days. If they don't hit by then, they won't hit at all. My money's on them tryin' one last time. Before the police put two and two together."

"Mind if I join the party?"

"It's a free country," I said. "The casino's open to everyone. Even Gaming Control."

TWENTY-FOUR

SINCE I WAS already downtown, I decided to head to the police station and see what Queeney had discovered, if anything. After my encounter with Bentley, I wasn't sure I could rely on what he'd told me. My connections to the underworld, little as they were, seemed to cast over him a shadow of doubt. Not that I could blame him. He knew little about me, and I the same about him. It was a heck of a way to establish trust. Besides, I needed to tell Queeney about Keys. Not that I wanted to drop a dime on the guy, but it would be better that he heard it from me.

I parked outside, went into the station, and found the detective bureau. Queeney was a lieutenant, which meant he had his own office, complete with his name—Lieutenant Connor McQueeney—on the door, to help him find the place. It wasn't much to speak of, little more than a desk, a file cabinet, and two chairs, all of which were brand spanking new in 1930. The most modern thing was the black phone sitting on the desk. Its thick cord trailing off the side, disappearing somewhere between the desk and the wall. The walls themselves were smartly decorated with photos of wanted men, a certificate of some type nestled in the middle. Queeney was sitting at his desk. His Stacy Adams and his suit coat both resting on a coat hanger in the corner. He looked up at me as I entered.

"Max Rossi," he said. "Come to turn yourself in?"

"Hardly." I removed my lid and took an unoffered seat, hoping it still had enough life for at least one more sitting. "I have some information that may be of interest."

Queeney raised his thick, red brows. "Oh," he said. "What might that be?"

The chair squealed under Queeney's weight as he leaned back. He was built like a linebacker; a man who made everything on his desk appear smaller than it really was. He probably could've played for Boston College, if he hadn't been born with the family curse. Police officers tended to pass their badges down to their sons, each generation trying to live up to the mystique of the one before—whether deserved or not. But who was I to talk?

As with most families, the McQueeneys had skeletons in their closet—family members on the take. But his father wasn't one of them. That man was blue through and through. Enough that it cost him his life. Which is why Queeney the younger found himself in the high desert instead of his home turf by the sea. I guess I wasn't the only one running away from his future.

"I think I might know the source of that opium."

"Let me guess, Vincent 'Keys' Collins."

"Bentley called you already."

Queeney nodded. "That he did. Told me all about your meeting."

"That was fast," I said.

"So you really don't know where this Keys character is?"

"I really don't," I said. "But he's not my main concern right now. Keeping the Highwaymen from hitting the casino is."

"Shouldn't you be there then?"

"We're having a shindig tonight; thought you might want to make an appearance. You know, all coincidental-like."

Queeney scratched the scalp under his red hair. "What are you trying to pull?" he asked.

"Keys is missing. Dorsey, or whatever his name is, is dead. The Highwaymen have either already skedaddled or they're going to do the deed tonight and then take the run out. It could be the catch of a lifetime."

"And you want me there?"

I stood. "Oh, I don't want you there," I said and replaced my lid. "I don't really even know you. In fact, we aren't even having this conversation. But it's a free world and if some guy gets his elbows checked by some flatfoot who just happened to be in the casino minding his own beeswax, well, who's the wiser?"

I was headed to the door when Queeney stopped me.

"Hold on a second," he said. He shuffled the papers around on his desk, then shuffled them again just for fun. Finally, he pulled out a form and handed it to me. "Fill this out," he said.

I looked at the paper. Private Investigator's License was written in bold letters at the top.

"What's this about?"

"It's an application. Fill it out and bring it back with fifty bucks. If you really want to be out of the game, then get out with both feet," he said. "Now go away. Unless you're going to confess to a crime, I have work to do.

I tipped my hat and left.

TWENTY-FIVE

MY NEXT STOP was the El Rancho. I was hoping to find the dealer Keys spoke with the other night. There was still a chance that Keys wasn't involved in this whole thing. Of course, there was also a chance that Virginia was going to forgive my stupidity, but that chance was fat, and not in a good way. I parked, tossed the attendant two bits, and headed inside.

The dealer was in the third pit I came to on a twenty-one table with five seats—all of them occupied by four people. Just my luck. He was wearing the same Western-style suit as before, his shirt decorated with a black string bowtie. I squeezed myself between a man too large for his chair and a woman in a button-down blouse and red cat-eye frames; the corners decorated with small rhinestones. Her brown, shoulder-length hair was pulled back and held in place with a similarly colored ribbon.

The large man had squeezed himself into a suit that must have shrunk in the rain, had there been any. His lid, which was meant for a much smaller man, rested on the table to his right, and his tie looked as if it would give way at any moment.

He adjusted himself onto one chair, trying to find a balance for his sizable girth. I laid two fins on the table and waited for the hand to end. When it did, the dealer took my bills and replaced them with ten white chips. He shuffled the deck and started to deal. Twenty-one, or blackjack as it is called, is a game of luck and all of it rests with the house. The only way to win is to have an unexplainable streak or to cheat in some manner. The latter of which is heavily frowned upon in the finer establishments.

The object of the game, as the name suggests, is to get as close to twenty-one as possible without going over. It doesn't matter how many cards you take to do it, so long as you don't go over twenty-one. This game is played against the house, and each player has an equal chance of losing. Everyone gets two cards face up, except the dealer who gets one face up and one face down. Because you're playing the house—that is, the dealer—it doesn't matter who sees your cards and bluffing isn't necessary. This also keeps the player's hands off the cards and reduces the likelihood of gaining you a visit by a couple of men with crooked noses.

Each player can take as many hits as wanted until one of three things happens: you hit twenty-one, in which case you win; you go over twenty-one, in which case you lose; or you decide to hold at the number of your choice. Face cards are the value on the face, royalty is worth ten, and an ace is either eleven or one, your choice, unless you're the dealer, then it's always an eleven. The dealer goes last. He turns over his card and if the total is sixteen or under, he must take a card until he reaches at least seventeen. If the dealer shows a seventeen or higher, he must stand—that is, he gets no more cards. Simple, as long as you can count, and incredibly dull.

Unlike poker, there is no ante. A player is allowed to put as many chips as warms his or her little heart in the circle on the felt before the cards are even dealt. The odds are so in favor of the house, you'd think blackjack was invented by the mob.

The dealer gave the first card to the player two seats to my right. Setting it in front of him in an area called "the box." It was a jack. He then gave a three to the large man directly to my right. It was when he dealt me the nine that he first got a good look at me. It took only moments for the recognition to set in and his eyes to enlarge to twice their size. I smiled.

He quickly dealt two more cards to the players to my left—a five and a two. He gave himself a ten and started the circle again. He dealt with quivering hands, making sure to look at the cards, not the players. He gave the jack a six, the three a five, and me another nine. It was a nice pair, but pairs don't count in blackjack. Cat Eyes got another five and the last player got an eight.

The dealer turned back to the first player. He decided to stand on his sixteen, not the smartest move in the world, he should have hit. The odds were not in his favor. It was the large man's turn.

"Hit me," he said, and the dealer gave him a queen. He decided to stand.

When the dealer got to me, I split the pair, adding an equal amount of chips to the second card.

"Can you do that?" Cat Eyes asked me.

"I believe it's allowed," I said and looked toward the dealer.

"You can split any cards that are the same pair," he said, keeping his gaze directly on Cat Eyes.

"You just have to place the same bet on the second set of cards," I added.

He dealt me a king and a jack. I held on each pair.

Cat Eyes thought it would be fun to do the same. She split her fives and doubled the bet. I wouldn't have done that. Her two fives were a ten and very few cards in the deck can hurt a ten. She received an eight and a seven for her troubles. Now she had thirteen and twelve, but would have had eighteen. She took a hit on the thirteen, received a three, and took another. She took one more hit, like a smart girl, and got another three. Now she had nineteen and was sitting pretty. She took a hit on the twelve and was dealt a queen—twenty-two. The dealer took her chips and the cards from her losing had, leaving the other in the box.

"Well, at least I have one hand still," she said with a smile.

I smiled back. She clearly thought she had broken even, not realizing she had already lost one hand and was now behind.

Cat Eyes seemed to be friends with the last player, a female, because they both screamed and hugged each other when the dealer dealt her an ace—twenty-one. The dealer paid her and removed her cards from the table. Then the dealer turned over his face-down card, revealing a seven. He had to stand on his seventeen, which means the large man, Cat Eyes, and I all won the hands we had in play. The girls yelled out again. The large man and I did not.

The dealer dealt several more hands, his own getting shakier as he went. At one point the pit boss came and asked him if he was all right. He assured the man he was. I wasn't convinced. I waited until all but Cat Eyes and her companion had left the table. I would have waited for them to leave too, but they seemed to be in no hurry to do so.

"Remember me?" I asked as the dealer shuffled.

"I don't believe I do," he said, without taking his eyes off the cards.

"Really? Cause I was just in here two days ago with a friend of yours. Keys Collins."

I could see the blood leave his face. To his credit, he recovered quickly.

"I'm sure you're mistaken, sir," he said.

"Oh, I don't think so. I'm pretty good with faces. My friend Dorsey was as well. Maybe you know him. He went by Slater when he played here."

The dealer pushed the shuffled cards in front of Cat Eyes. "Please cut the deck," He said to her.

I reached up and grabbed his wrist. Cat Eyes jerked her hand back. He tried to pull away, but I didn't let him. He was about to say something, but I spoke up first. "Go ahead," I said. "Call out. Get the pit boss' attention. Let's see what he knows about the suite with the dead man in it." He just looked at me, fear beginning to take hold.

The girls scooted away.

"Where's Keys?" I asked.

"I don't know what you're talking about."

"Sure you do." I turned his arm and pulled up his sleeve. Tracks followed his veins—some healed, some still fresh.

My actions caught the pit boss' attention. I let the dealer go. He pulled down his shirt sleeve.

"Excuse me, sir," the pit boss said. "But you are not allowed to handle the cards."

I stood. "I was just leaving," I said.

I left the dealer to the pit boss and walked to the other side of the casino. I sat in front of a slot machine, pretended to play, and waited. The two men spoke for a bit, then the dealer clapped his hands and waved them to show they were empty. As he made his way out of the pit to the employee area, he loosened his tie.

I jumped up and headed to valet. I passed the attendant a fin hoping it would encourage his feet to move faster. It did the trick. I slipped in behind the steering wheel and headed to the rear of the property. I parked at the back of the employee parking area and waited. I'd hoped my little stunt would unnerve the dealer enough to check out early.

It took only a few minutes before a tieless dealer came out of the back entrance, got into a Ford Crestline Sunliner, probably a '53, and pointed it off property. I put my own vehicle in gear and followed.

TWENTY-SIX

I FOLLOWED THE dealer as he headed north on Highway 91, passing both San Francisco Street and Charleston Boulevard toward downtown. When he got to Fremont, he turned left and headed up four streets before turning right on First Street and then taking another onto Stewart. If he was worried about being followed, he didn't show it. He headed straight for his destination, taking no side streets or detours that I could tell. It didn't surprise me; he seemed a man intent to get where he was going.

The dealer pulled up in front of a cottage-style house that looked like it might have been ordered from the Sears and Roebuck Catalog. It had a steep shingled roof with an oversized dormer smack in the middle. Stairs led to an inviting front porch, framed with columns on either side; two equally inviting rocking chairs sat motionless, awaiting occupants to bring them to life.

I took a spot three cars behind the dealer and waited

as he slid out of the driver's seat and headed up the porch stairs. I jumped from my car, pulled out my .38, and snuck over to the stairs, staying as low as I could get. I waited as he rang the front bell and when the door opened, I shot up the stairs and pushed myself into the dealer, forcing him inside the house.

The force threw him into the woman who had opened the door. She was a dark-skinned brunette clothed in a one-piece merry widow; stockings connected to clips at the bottom. She wore a frilly see-through, short-sleeved drape that hung low, past her knees and high, fuzzy heels. She almost fell when the dealer crashed into her.

"Hey, what's the meaning of this?" she called out.

"Where's Keys?" I asked. I closed the door behind me and positioned my .38 to get my point across.

"What are you talking about?" the woman said, trying to regain her composure.

"I don't have much time," I said. "This lug was in cahoots with the man I'm looking for. And now he's come here. To whatever this place is?"

The woman flashed the dealer a stern look. He lowered his head. "Perhaps 'lug,' is not a fit description," she said. I don't think she meant it as a compliment.

She pulled her drape closed and tried not to look at the gun. "Can I ask your name?"

"My name isn't important," I said.

"It's Rossi," the dealer offered. "I heard Keys..."

"Be quiet," she barked at him before he could finish.

We were standing in a plain foyer decorated with only a small table and one of those lamps that had tassels dangling from the shade. A flight of stairs headed upward to the right.

"Seeing as you're not here to rob the place, and since you aren't a cop, might I suggest we retreat to the sitting room?" the woman asked, sweet as sugar.

The dealer tried a step closer, but I motioned him back with the barrel. He took to scratching his arm.

"I'm fine right here," I said. I took a glance up the stairs. "Keys up there?" I asked, motioning with my head.

She didn't answer.

"Look, sister, we both know you're familiar with Keys, and, as you said, I'm not a cop. I just need to find him before the bluebottles do."

"Perhaps you could put your gun down," she said, pointing to the pistol. "It's making me nervous. Those things have a habit of going off. Buster here can get us a drink. Do you enjoy spiced rum?"

The dealer looked at her strangely. She gave him stern eyes.

"I think we're all just fine right here where we are," I said. I caught a glimpse of the next room, the sitting room. It was decorated mostly in shades of red with high back winged Chesterfields and Chaise lounges, complete with red button-tufted upholstery. Tall floor lamps, each with a tasseled shade, were positioned about the room near end tables that matched the chairs, lounge, and coffee tables. It looked nothing like the outside. Then it hit me.

"Is this a disorderly house?" I asked.

The woman looked as if she had just smelled something foul. "Certainly not," she said. This is a boarding house. A place women new to town can come and settle in. I assure you my girls are of the utmost character."

"And you're the house marm?" I asked.

"I am," she confirmed.

"Always answer the door in your undergarments?"

She drew the ties on the wrap around to her front and secured them in a loose bow. "How I answer my own door, is none of your concern."

"So this is where the roundheels came from," I said. "I thought all these were shut down."

"All those are. This is simply a female boarding house," she repeated. "Nothing more."

"Then why was Keys here?" I asked.

She fell silent.

"I'm going to ask you one more time, and then I'm going to lose my patience," I said.

It was at that moment that the front door yanked open; the knob hitting me square in the back. A mountain of a man, one who barely fit in the frame, forced himself inside. It was Vito, the larger of Sal's two shadows. Before I could react, he took hold of my wrist and squeezed it with all his might—a considerable amount. He wanted me to drop the gun. I didn't feel like complying. I tried to pull away, but no soap. I tried prying his fingers loose but hadn't thought to bring my crowbar. I tried to scrape my foot across his shin, but he moved his leg just in time. He wasn't as stupid as he looked.

After a moment, my fingers lost their feeling and the thing fell to the floor. The Mountain kicked it away, and the woman scooped it up. I looked up at the Mountain. He smiled, twisted my wrist, then introduced his knuckles to my face. Blood gushed from my nose. I tried to counter, but he grabbed my other wrist.

"This is payback," he said and lifted his knee into my crotch.

Fireworks went off and stars began to circle around my head. I was suddenly sick to my stomach. He followed the trick with two consecutive punches to the breadbasket and two more to my face, just for fun.

He held me up by my collar. "You got no business being here," he said. "This is Mr. Manella's place and he don't like you."

I assured him the feeling was mutual. He didn't take to the comment or my suggestion of what his mother did for a living and he showed it with two hard slaps across the face. I tried an uppercut but connected only with air.

"You got his gat?" he asked the woman.

She held it out. The Mountain took it and slid it into the pocket of his jacket. Then he opened the front door and threw me out of it. I landed with a thud on the porch. He came out and took hold of me again, then tossed me like a rag down the stairs onto the sidewalk.

"Don't ever come back here," he said.

I don't know what would make him think I'd want to.

TWENTY-SEVEN

I LAID ON the cool concrete until my head stopped pounding. I would have stood, but I couldn't yet feel my legs. I wasn't sure they could support me anyway. A stray dog came and sniffed my way, then thought better of it. When the earth stopped spinning, I rolled over to the curb and threw up in the street. After several minutes I was able to get to my knees and after several more, I could stand. I found my lid, made my way to my Roadmaster, using the other cars for support, got inside, and just sat there. The blood had returned to my hand and it was tingling with the feet of a thousand ants.

The dealer hadn't come out of the house, and neither had the Mountain. I didn't suppose they would until I drove away. But I was in no condition to drive. Luckily, my house wasn't too far. I brought the beast to life and pulled out of the spot, hoping, like Trigger, it knew the way home. I went slowly down Stewart to Seventh Street, passing out only once at a red light, but just until the horns behind me brought me back to life.

I stumbled inside the house and into my bedroom. I wanted to sleep. My head wanted me to sleep too, but the envelope made too much racket to let me rest. I pulled off my jacket and tie and laid them on the bed. Then I unbuttoned my blood-stained shirt, slipped off my shoes and socks, dropped my drawers, and headed for the bathroom. I draped my shirt from a hook on the wall inside the shower and turned the water on hot. Then I sat down on the toilet, rested my head against the wall, and waited until steam filled the room.

The water had been running for quite some time when I finally woke back up. I tried to stand, but my legs had fallen asleep and I hit the ground. The shower was only inches away, so I decided to crawl. I climbed into the tub and let the water hit me in the face. It was hot and it helped to wake me. I managed to get to my feet, slipping only twice, and cooled the water down to something that wasn't scorching.

I brought my hand to my nose and moved it around to make sure nothing was broken. I'd gotten lucky. My lip was split in two, but it would heal. After a while I washed my face, and the rest of me as well.

When I was all clean and ready to face the world again, I had a look in the mirror. It wasn't a pretty sight. My lip was not only split down the center, it was blown up like a Macy's Thanksgiving Day balloon. Bruises were also beginning to form and my right cheek was tender enough that I didn't let myself touch it. I made a right rube of myself, letting Vito get the better of me like that without even landing a single punch. What would the boys in the gym say? But I have to admit, his first hit rang my bell but good. After that, he might as well have been punching a side of beef for all the good I was.

I pulled a starched shirt from the drawer, chose another suit, and matched a tie to it, along with a square.

I didn't put on my shoulder holster, because I didn't want it to get lonely without a gun. I would've asked the Mountain for it back, but I had a feeling it wouldn't have gone well. As I dressed, I wondered if Keys really was hiding in that house, and if he wasn't, why did that dealer go there? And if Keys wasn't there, where was he?

I found my lid, placed it where it belonged, and headed out the door, ignoring the envelope's laughter. I needed to get back to the Sands and see what I could do to stop the Highwaymen from hitting the place, if they, in fact, planned to do just that. I hopped in the Roadmaster, hoping my feet would still work enough to manage the pedals. They did. I drove north to Charleston, then headed west to Fifth Street.

I had gone about a block and a half when I noticed a bar I'd not remembered seeing. Honestly, it wasn't surprising. I'd been spending far too much time at the Sands and not enough walking around my own neighborhood. And while I needed to get there, this particular bar enticed me enough that I turned around. I found a parking spot and went inside the El Bailarín Pirata.

The place was mostly empty except for a couple of men nursing drinks at the bar. My father would have called this a dive bar and he would have been right. It was a tiny hole in the wall decorated with the trappings of a seafarer—nets, buoys, mermaids with fishtails and shells for tops; though how they stayed there was a mystery. All manner of rum sat on the shelves behind the bar, most of it imported from Jamaica or Puerto Rico.

The bartender came over. He was a brute of a man, one that would have come in handy earlier in the evening. I ordered a manhattan, then changed it to Ron Del Barrilito when his face told me it was a better option.

"How long has this place been here?" I asked.

"'Bout ten years now," he said as he poured my drink.

"Interesting place," I said.

The bartender huffed. "It'll do in a pinch."

He passed me my rum and I took a sip. It stung when it touched my lip, but I got used to it. I wasn't a rum man, but this could have converted me. It went down smooth, as any good drink should. Of course, that could have just been the bruises talking.

"You the owner?" I asked.

"No, I just tend bar." He looked at me intently. "You get the plate of the bus that ran you over?"

I tried to smile, but nothing was working. "I'm afraid it's a bus with which I'm all too familiar."

The bartender began drying glasses as bartenders do.

"Interesting name for a bar," I said.

He laughed. "Yeah, the owner was a big fan of the movie."

"You lost me there," I admitted.

"El Bailarín Pirata. The Dancing Pirate. Came out in '36. The movie poster is over there on the wall," he said, pointing behind me.

I stood and walked over to the poster, taking my drink with me for company. The musical, The Dancing Pirate, had indeed come out in 1936. It starred Charles Collins as Jonathan Pride, who was captured and taken to Spain. *Collins*, I thought to myself and wondered if Keys' father had seen the movie as well. The colorful poster, which promoted the movie being made in Technicolor, featured a man and woman dancing what was probably the rhumba or maybe the lambada. Who knew? The man looked no more like a pirate than I did a gentleman.

I took another drink and stared at the poster some more and that's when the fog seemed to lift. Pirata was pirate in Spanish. I slammed down the rest of the rum, placed the glass and two singles on the bar, then headed for the Sands.

TWENTY-EIGHT

I PLACED MY Roadmaster in its spot and headed inside to the front desk. I picked up a phone and called Charlie.

"Anything yet?" I asked.

"Nothing," he said. "But we're keeping a close eye on everything."

"You bring the pit bosses up to speed?"

Charlie assured me he had and added that he'd informed security as well. When I hung up, I called Fingers but got no answer. I called the Whirlaway Suite and got the same result, so I headed to the tables to see if we'd been joined by any of Las Vegas' finest. The casino was unusually full for a Monday night. Queeney was sitting at one of the tables, looking very much like a cop. Bentley was also there, though he managed to be a little harder to spot. He stood, chips in hand, behind a craps table, eyeing the players. He caught my eye and gave me a discrete nod.

I found a house phone and called Charlie back. When he answered, I told him about Queeney and Bentley, giving him a description of Bentley and telling him they were here to help. I also told him to keep it on the Q.T. for the time being. Charlie agreed.

I went over to a pit boss to inquire about Fingers' whereabouts and was told he was in the Emerald Room, so I headed up the stairs. I opened the door and found an armed security officer standing guard in the typical police-style uniform. "I need to see Mr. Abbandandolo," I said.

"Wait here," the man told me.

He walked over to Fingers, who was playing poker with a group of business associates, one of them I recognized as Charles Duncan Baker, mayor of Las Vegas—C.D. to his friends. He was clad in a white shirt, his tie loosened and his top button undone, a cigar firmly clamped between his teeth. He barked out his disapproval of the dealer.

"Confound it, man! Don't you have any good cards in that deck?"

There were two other men, and two other cigars, but I didn't recognize them. A waitress was also there, bringing the men food and drink, and whatever else they desired. The security officer said his piece to Fingers, who then turned and motioned for me to enter. I walked over to the table.

"Sorry to bother you, but I have news," I said.

C.D. turned to me. He pulled the cigar from his mouth and let out a whistle. "You look like hell, son," he said. "Who put you through the meat grinder?"

"Don't worry," I said, "it's what all the cool kids are doing."

I couldn't tell if I had confused or annoyed the man.

"Excuse me, gentlemen," Fingers said. "I have business to attend."

So that's what gentlemen looked like.

"You expect us to wait?" C.D. asked, "Or are you folding?"

Fingers threw his cards on the table, face up, revealing a strong three of a kind. "Here you go," he said. "Merry Christmas."

We went to the back of the room, near the small bar. Fingers took the white couch facing the players and I sat in the high back chair, my back to them. The Emerald Room, true to its name, was green. Green carpet, green wallpaper, green trim on the white chairs. Curtains covered non-existent windows and lights made to look like candelabras rested atop half columns protruding from the walls. It was a special room and you had to be somebody to get inside. I'd been here a couple of times.

"C.D.'s right, you do look like hell. This seems to be a pattern of yours."

More than he realized.

"You want a drink?" Fingers asked.

"Sure," I said. I walked to the bar, got two glasses and a bottle of Old Forester. I poured Fingers a respectable amount and doubled it for myself.

Fingers pulled an ashtray over and rolled the tip of the cigar inside. "This better be good," he said. "You cost me a nice hand."

"Oh, it's good," I said and took a quick swig. "I think I've found the leader of the Highwaymen and she's been under our noses the entire time."

That got his attention.

"She?" he asked.

"Elizabeth 'Lizzie' Averill, a.k.a. Veronica Penn. Daughter of Walter 'Pirata' Penn, last known leader of the Highwaymen."

Fingers' eyes hardened. "How do you know this?" he asked.

"One of the times I took Lizzie out, she told me her father was a pirate."

"That doesn't prove anything," Fingers said.

"On its own, yes, but there's other evidence. I was in the suite once and found a suitcase in Lizzie's closet. It was a small suitcase, something you'd give a kid. I didn't think much of it at first, but when I found Pirata Penn had a daughter named Veronica, I remembered the suitcase had the initials VP, which could stand for Veronica Penn. Then when Dorsey was playing once, he called Lizzie 'Ronnie.' As a kid I had a friend with an older sister named Veronica, her friends all called her Ronnie. Plus I saw a photo of her mother. There's definitely a resemblance. She lied to me once about her whereabouts, and we were at the El Rancho the night Dorsey was murdered; only Lizzie didn't want to be there."

"Where is she now?"

"I don't know. I've got Charlie watching the games in case the Highwaymen hit tonight. I called the suite but got no answer. I wanted to tell you first, before I took any action."

Fingers took several puffs while studying the ceiling. I poured myself another drink so the first wouldn't be lonely and waited. After a moment he spoke.

"Get to the suite and see if she's there," he said. "If she's not there and she hasn't checked out, then wait for her to arrive. If she's there or she has checked out, call me here." Fingers called to the waitress. "Get me a phone," he said.

The waitress brought a phone over to Fingers, stretching the cord across the entire room. He picked up the receiver.

I stood, downed the last of my drink, then left. On my way down the stairs, I was greeted by several women dressed as if they were going to a pajama party. They were followed by Salvatore Manella.

"Well, don't you look like hell?" he said with a chuckle.

I wanted to wipe the chuckle off his smug kisser, but it wasn't the time. Instead, I threw my arm against the opposite wall, blocking his progress.

"Get your arm out of my face!" Sal ordered. He gave me the mobster stare. I think they taught it during the blood oath, or maybe they learned it from the nuns. What did I know?

"When this is all over," I said, leaning in, "you and I are gonna settle this. Mano a Mobster."

Sal moved even closer. "Get your arm out of the way," he said intently.

I didn't see it at first. Not until it caught the light from the stairwell. The barrel was only inches from my midsection. It was a fine piece, one that had chosen Sal's side. Who was I to argue? I lowered my arm.

Sal smiled. "Anytime, Junior," he said. "Anytime."

I stood and watched as he went up the stairs and into the Emerald Room.

TWENTY-NINE

I HEADED INTO the casino to find Bentley. He was hovering around a roulette table, watching the players bet. I slipped in behind him.

"Any action on this table?"

"Not much to speak of," he said while keeping his eye on the players. Then added, "You walk into a wall?"

"Close," I said. "You got a minute?"

He nodded.

"I'll be by the five-dollar machines," I said.

Bentley joined me a few minutes later. "I think I figured out who's leading the Highwaymen," I said.

"Oh?"

"I think it's the daughter. Veronica Penn."

Bentley looked at me and shook his head. "That can't be possible," he said. "She went into hiding after her father was killed. She hasn't been heard of for years."

"So you don't know where she is?"

He admitted he didn't.

"Or what she looks like," I added.

"Is she here in the casino?"

"I don't know. She came in with our whale; played the girlfriend. Kept me away from the place while he scoped it out. Led me by the nose."

I told Bentley everything I had told Fingers, leaving out a few key facts, like the name of the suite, and as I did, my mind drifted to a panther head bracelet.

"You still with me?" Bentley asked.

"You know," I said. "There was a time when she took me into a jewelry store on a lark. We pretended I was going to buy her something and she slipped a bracelet into my pocket without me knowing, then stormed out of the store, leaving me to a nice charge of larceny and burglary. She didn't even stick by to tell them it was just a joke."

Bentley nodded. "Sounds like she was testing you."

"What do you mean?"

"She wanted to see if you could get yourself out of a pinch."

I thought about that for a minute. It's not like my position here was common knowledge. She may have been told I was a house dick but wanted to find out for herself. Maybe she wanted to make sure she had the right man. It was beginning to make sense.

"I'm going to check her suite."

"I'll go with you."

"I'd prefer you didn't," I said. "Let me make sure she's there and then I'll give you and Queeney a heads up."

"He the big Irishman at the twenty-one table?"

I laughed.

"Sticks out like a black eye," he said.

I agreed.

"Okay," Bentley said. "Your property, your way."

My next stop was the front desk. I asked about the Whirlaway Suite, specifically if anyone had yet checked out. I was told they hadn't, so I headed there. I rang the doorbell, then rang it again when no one answered. I got lucky on the second try when Lizzie came to the door. She wore a short-sleeved, uniform style dress, with a belt around the center. The scarf around her neck was held in place with a jeweled broach. Her hair was combed back and covered with a round pillbox hat. The jewelry clipped to her ears matched the broach. Gloves rested next to her purse on the table. Traveling clothes.

"Oh, Maxie," she said. "What happened to you?" She reached over and took my face in her hands. It smarted, causing me to pull back. "Does it hurt?"

"A bit," I said. "But I'll be all right."

"Have you been in a fight?"

"If you can call it that," I said.

"Please, come in."

I followed her inside. Two suitcases sat on the floor of the entryway; her coat draped over the tops.

"Going somewhere?" I asked.

"Well I can't stay here forever," she said. "I didn't pay for the room and I certainly can't afford to keep it."

We walked into the main room. She turned, put her arms around my neck, and kissed me gently on the cheek.

"It's just one for the road," she said. "Come, let's have a drink and toast our time together."

She walked over to the bar.

"How are you getting home?" I asked.

"Oh, I found a bit of money tucked away in Dorsey's things. I'm sure he won't mind." She took two glasses from the shelf on the bar and laid them on the counter. "Ice," she said. "We need ice." Then disappeared underneath the bar.

I took the opportunity to look about the place. It was much cleaner and tidier than the last time I'd been here. Not a panty out of place. "Then you're headed back to California?" I asked.

She poked her head up. "Oh, I'm not sure. I've been thinking about a change of pace. I hear New Orleans is nice." She disappeared again with the two glasses, popping up a moment later with the same glasses, only this time they were filled with ice. She poured a brown alcohol into them and brought them over to the sitting area.

"Have a seat," she said.

I took the couch and Lizzie sat next to me, curling her legs underneath herself. She held her glass up for a toast. "To us," she said. "We could have been great."

I relented and clinked my glass to hers. She brought the glass to her red lips and took a sip. I did the same, only my red lips weren't the result of lipstick. The alcohol stung, just as it had before, but it didn't stop me. I could feel the sweat forming on the back of my neck and wondered if this was going to happen every time I went into a suite at the Sands. But this time it felt different. The room seemed stuffy, as if someone had let out all the air.

"Maybe we should open a window," I said.

Lizzie smiled. She put her drink on the coffee table and came over to me. She removed my lid and placed it on the table. "You know, Maxie," she said as she loosened my tie, "you're one tough nut to crack." She undid my top button. I wanted to stop her, but my arms seemed to not be working anymore.

"I tried everything to get to you." She took my drink and set it on the table. Then she took my feet and swung them up on the couch.

"What are...you..."

"Shhhh," she said. "Don't try to talk now. She unlaced my shoes and removed them from my feet. Another man entered the room. He looked familiar, but I couldn't quite see him. He had gloves on.

"Just drape them over the lampshades and the backs of the chairs," Lizzie said to him. "Then get those bottles from under the counter and lay them on the floor. Take the dirty glasses behind the bar and scatter them around."

I watched as the man placed what looked like bras and panties around the room. It was getting hard to focus.

"You know," Lizzie said, "at first I was thinking about recruiting you. It would help to have a man on the inside, especially if that man was a house dick. But you're a clever one, aren't you? You had to go figure everything out. I bet you even know my real name, don't you?"

"Virginia," I said, the word coming out like tree sap in the winter.

"That's right, Maxie." She pulled off my socks, loosened my belt, and unzipped my slacks.

The man came up behind her. "You ready for the stuff?" he asked.

I got a good look at the man. "Hollis," I said with a thick tongue.

"That's right," Lizzie said. "He was our inside man," but stupid Dorsey had to go and ruin that.

"You killed him," I said.

"Well of course, silly," Lizzie said. "He got too big for

his britches and those sex parties were just getting to be too much. I knew I never should have chosen him. Oh well, it doesn't matter now."

A voice told her that she'd never get away with it. It sounded like my voice, but I wasn't sure.

"Oh pish posh," she said. "Of course I'll get away with it. You're a drug addict, Maxie. You're even friends with a dealer. Lots of people have seen you two together. You just took one too many. It happens all the time."

Hollis came out of the back room with something in his hand. Lizzie rolled up my sleeve and tied something around my bicep. "Too bad," she said. "You really are a cute one. I could have gotten sweet for you."

Hollis handed her what looked like a syringe. She pushed the needle in my arm. "Sleep well, Maxie," she said. "Sleep well."

As the room started to spin, I wondered if she had said those words to Dorsey.

THIRTY

I RAN AROUND the corner, but it was too close behind me. I could hear its roars, see its emerald eyes. It was coming after me. I ran into the main room and flung open the curtain. There was a woman on the other side of the glass. A ragged wedding dress hung from her like draperies in an abandoned building. She had holes all down her front; blood coming from each one. She pulled out a tommy gun from behind her and started shooting. I dove behind the couch.

A thick envelope rested on the floor. It moved closer to me. I heard someone laugh. Just then the panther came around the end of the couch. He was crouched low and moving steadily toward me. I scooted backward on my heels and the palms of my hands, but step by step, the panther kept coming. It bared its teeth. They were big and yellow and looked like they could easily bite through a leg or an arm. I kept moving backward. The panther kept coming. The laughter got louder.

I backed up as far as I could go, stopping when I hit a cabinet or a wall. I couldn't tell. The panther came so close, I could feel its hot, moist breath on my skin. It smelled like death. With its teeth only inches from my face, it roared loudly. I turned away. Suddenly it lifted its paw and slapped me hard across the face. Before I could react, it slapped me again.

"Wake up, Max," it said. "You have to wake up." Then it slapped me a third time. I opened my eyes. A blur of a man was standing above me. "Wake up!" he yelled.

I looked up at the ceiling. The panther was there, looking down at me with emerald eyes, holding the envelope. I pointed to the ceiling so the blurry man could see it too. He turned and looked up.

"You're hallucinating, Max. There's nothing there," the man said.

I blinked and looked again. The panther was gone, and he'd taken the envelope with him. I concentrated on the man, forcing my eyes to look at him until he came into focus. He was a familiar man. A man for whom I had been searching. A man who sold opium.

The man brought me a glass of cold water. I thought he wanted me to drink it, but he didn't. He wanted me to wear it and showed that, as he pulled his arm back and threw it into my face. It took my breath.

He held something under my nose. "Take a snort," he ordered. "A deep, long snort."

I did as I was told. The smell permeated my nostrils and burned. I was almost immediately sick to my stomach. The man pulled me from the couch and made me stand. I tried to fall back down, but he wouldn't let me. Someone had snuck into my head and was beating the drums. Jungle drums. Perhaps they were calling the panther.

There was a strong odor of whiskey. The good kind.

The kind you drink in a classy joint with a special girl or friends. It was coming from me.

The man pulled me into the bathroom, tossed me in the shower, and turned the water on cold. I think I screamed out, but the man held my head under the water. I worried about my clothes, then realized I wasn't wearing them. After several moments I was able to catch my breath. I pushed his hand away and braced myself against the wall, letting the water bring me back to life. It felt like I'd been here before.

The man left. When I felt I could stand without the wall to brace me, I turned off the shower and wrapped myself in a towel. The drums were still in my head, only now a fog had gathered there as well. It was a thick fog, the kind that swept into Boston Harbor in the winter, obscuring the boats and disorienting captains.

Keys came back into the bathroom. He had a glass in his hand. "Drink this," he said.

I groped in the fog for the glass. Keys steadied my hands. "What is it?" I asked.

"Water. With a little Bromo-Seltzer. It'll help settle your stomach. I'm afraid you're in for a session of vomiting."

Great, I thought and took the glass. "What did you give me?"

"Don't worry about that," he said. "Just be glad I found you when I did."

I drank Keys' offering. It had a nasty flavor, but was better than what I had inhaled previously. I asked him the obvious question. "How did you find me?"

He waited a moment before he answered. "I didn't kill that man," he said. "I know it looks like I did, but I didn't."

"You sold him the opium," I said.

Keys shook his head. "I never even met the guy."

"Then how did he get your business card?"

"I don't have any idea."

"Do you give those out often?" I asked.

"Sure," Keys said. "Everyone I do business with."

"Business?" I questioned.

He lifted his lid and scratched his head.

I tried to encourage him. "You might as well spill it at this point. I know you're selling and that you have warrants out for you. How much worse can it be?"

Keys hunched his shoulders. "All right. I guess the jig is up." He took a deep breath. "I run hop and sex parties," he said. "I get an employee to get us a room, then recruit Joes to join the party. I supply the drugs."

"And the roundheels?"

"You stay in town long enough, you make connections. Ms. Delilah is one of those connections. It's symbiotic, man." He grew stern. "But I don't kill anyone, and no one is forced to do anything they don't already want to."

I was continually surprised at what people were able to justify. Keys was committing a crime and he knew it, but the fact that the participants in this little rendezvous of his were willing and able made everything square in his eyes. He was simply supplying a service. No harm. No foul.

"What was with that dealer then? The one from the El Rancho."

Keys studied the floor, then looked up. "He was my inside man. I had a fix on a big score that was to be delivered to one of the hotel rooms. He was supposed to help, but got cold feet." His eyes grew cold and he stiffened. "He was also stealing from me. That's what I get for working with a user."

Keys looked like he was telling the truth. He didn't

have trouble keeping eye contact and he wasn't fiddling with his hands. If Keys didn't supply the drugs, it was likely the dealer was making a little cabbage on the side. Since he had little problem rubbing elbows with the criminal element, he was probably the inside man for the Highwaymen as well. In fact, it was probably the dealer at the El Rancho who passed the card on to Lizzie and it was probably the dealer who sold her the drugs. The suite was a setup just like this one was supposed to be.

"You ever have one of those parties in this suite?" I asked.

Keys shook his head. "This is the first time I've ever been in this suite."

"Did Dorsey ever attend one of them?"

"That the guy from the El Rancho?" Keys asked.

I told him it was.

He shook his head again. "I told you, I never met the guy."

I walked over to the phone and asked PBX to connect me with surveillance. Charlie answered. "Charlie, it's Max. Is that overgrown Irishman still sitting at the twenty-one table?"

"Yeah," Charlie said.

"Call the pit and have the pit boss tell him to meet me in the Whirlaway Suite. Tell him to bring Bentley."

Keys took out a cigarette and lit it.

"Where's my clothes?" I asked.

Keys nodded to the main room. I headed there. He followed.

"You never told me how you found me," I said.

"Heard you were looking for me," Keys said. "Ms. Delilah told me you paid her a visit and that it didn't go well. The dealer and I had a talk." He paused. "He told me everything...eventually."

I pulled on my shirt and slacks and tightened the belt. I looked at Keys hands, his knuckles told me he'd been in a fight. Likely one-sided.

Keys blew a puff in the air.

I wrapped my tie around my neck and began the knot. "You'd better take it on the heel before the hammer and saws get here," I said. "I don't know if they have photos of you, but I don't want to try and explain what you're doing here." I nodded to the sliding glass door. "You can take the back way out."

Keys smiled. He put out his smoke and threw on his cheaters. "You're one cool cat," he said and offered me his hand. "I hope our paths cross again."

I took his hand, but I wasn't sure how I felt about the rest.

THIRTY-ONE

QUEENEY WAS NONE too pleased when he got to the room. After I told him what had happened, he chided me like I'd broken his favorite pint glass. Bentley wasn't any better.

"And you let her get away." Queeney stated more than asked.

"I was a bit incapacitated at the time," I said.

"So you don't know where she's headed?" Queeney asked. I think steam was rising from his collar. Of course, I could have still been hallucinating.

"I told you, she said she was headed to New Orleans, but I doubt she was telling the truth."

"You should have let me come with you," Bentley said.

"I should have done a lot of things," I countered.

Queeney pulled out a toothpick and chewed on the end. "And this mystery man who helped you out?" he said. "You sure you don't know him?"

"I couldn't see straight," I explained. "I can barely see you now. He came in, made me sniff something, and dumped me in the shower. I'm lucky I didn't drown."

Queeney was skeptical. Bentley rode along with him.

"You gonna dust the room?" I asked.

"What for?" Queeney asked. "Here you are, lousy with excuses while everyone walked. If you ask me, there's something queer about all this."

"Let me see your arm," Bentley said.

"You buyin' his line?" I asked.

"Just roll it up," he said.

I rolled up my sleeve and showed Bentley the single puncture wound. The syringe and needle were still on the table where either Keys or Lizzie had left it.

"Could be self-inflicted," Bentley said, then pulled up my other sleeve. It was clean.

I pulled my arm away. "Yes, and all this was just a farce. Is that what you want to hear?" I asked as I pulled down my sleeves. "That I dragged the both of you to the Sands just to have my own private pipe and doxie party? And then call you down here when it was done, so I could look like some kind of hophead? The Highwaymen didn't strike. I told you they might or they might not. I didn't know. You took a chance as much as I did. It didn't pan out, that's all."

"Don't get starched," Queeney said. "This isn't the first time you've been the patsy to some dame."

"Well gee," I said. "The next time Lizzie tries to overdose me, I'll make sure she calls you first."

Queeney paused and took the toothpick out of his mouth. He examined the end before placing it back in. "Just leave everything as it is," he said. "I'll get the boys to sweep the room." He moved closer and towered above me. "I find out you're..."

He didn't finish the sentence. He didn't have to.

As Queeney walked out. Bentley stepped toward me. "You really should have let me come with you," he said.

I nodded.

"If you find anything, you'll let me know?"

I told him I would and he left. I really couldn't blame Queeney and I suppose I should have let Keys get what was coming to him, but I believed him when he told me he didn't kill Dorsey and he did save my life. He didn't have to come to the Sands. He put himself in jeopardy just doing it. It could have all been a setup and he would have walked right into it. But I would have died if he hadn't. He also stuck around to make sure I was jake. He didn't have to do that either.

Keys had put me back in touch with my musical self. Something I didn't realize I had been missing. But he was right; once the music is in your blood, man, it stayed there. A notion hit me. I'd never asked Keys how he got into the suite, but he was Keys after all—a man everybody liked. I'm sure he got security or, more likely, the night maid, to open it up for him.

Garwood was right, Keys was full of demons, yet he still managed to do the right thing in the end. Besides, a man with that many warrants will eventually get his comeuppance when the time is right. Things have a way of balancing themselves out. This just wasn't the right time.

I looked around the room. It was in the same condition it had been when I was here before with Lizzie. Empty bottles strewn around. Glasses half filled, some knocked over. Bras and panties hanging from the lampshades and furniture. One was even hanging from the drapes. It was a nice touch and I'd almost wished I'd attended the party. Lizzie had wanted me to see it that way. She'd already taken care of Dorsey but was setting the trap for me. I wondered if she'd planned to take me out, or if I was just an inconvenience she had to deal with at the last minute.

I found my lid on the carpet, under the coffee table. It had been stepped on. I straightened it out and laid it back on my head. I was about to leave, when I looked down and saw my toes wiggling back up at me. I found my shoes and socks, put them back where they belonged, and headed out the door.

I stopped at the front desk and informed them that the occupants of the Whirlaway Suite had checked out and that they needed to wait to clean the room until the police were finished. Then I called surveillance and checked in with Charlie. He gave the place a clean bill of health. It didn't surprise me.

I would have gone up to the Emerald Suite, but I figured Fingers and his crew were probably getting themselves acquainted with Sal's female friends, and I thought it best not to disturb them. Nothing had happened that couldn't wait until tomorrow morning. Besides, my stomach was sending me hate mail and I needed to get to a safe place as soon as possible, so I found my Roadmaster and let it take me home.

THIRTY-TWO

I WOKE UP the next morning after a long night of hugging the porcelain throne. I showered, shaved, and chose my favorite suit, hoping it would help me feel better than I looked. I picked up the suit I'd worn when dancing with the Mountain and checked it for valuables. The application Queeney had given me was still in the inside pocket. I slipped it into the same pocket of my new suit and placed the other suit, along with my shirt and slacks, into a dry cleaning bag I would drop off at the Sands.

The envelope had stopped laughing, so I got a chair, took off the cover, pulled the thing from the vent, and slipped it into the same pocket as the application. I replaced the cover, then headed for my Roadmaster. It seemed happier today as it headed down the road toward the Sands—or maybe it was just me. I put it in its spot and went upstairs to the mezzanine.

When I got there, Leona was at her desk. "Oh my,"

she said when she saw me. "What did you get yourself into?"

"I cheated on my girl and she slapped me," I said.

She stood and took hold of my chin. She turned me one way and then the other. "I'd say she did more than just slap you." She placed a soft hand against my cheek. "You going to be okay?" she asked.

"There's other loves," I said. "Perhaps you'll take pity on me."

"Don't count on it," she said and sat back down. "I suppose you want to see him."

I told her I did, and she showed me inside, only this time I turned down the manhattan. Fingers was sitting behind his desk, so I pulled over a chair and sat in front of it.

"I didn't hear from you last night," he said.

"I didn't have anything urgent to report and from the looks of things, I figured you didn't want to be disturbed."

"I'm guessing we didn't get hit then," he said.

I confirmed that we didn't, then told him everything that happened, leaving out Queeney and Bentley. What good would it do to bring them in?

"You okay?" he asked.

"I'm okay," I said. "It was a rough night, but I made it through."

"And Averill got away?"

"Yes," I said. "Along with Hollis, that dealer who used to work here. It appears he was indeed the inside man."

He nodded. It struck me as strange that he didn't seem terribly upset Lizzie or Hollis had gotten away, or that I hadn't called him sooner.

"Why don't you take a couple days off," he said. "It looks like you could use it."

How right he was.

I stood. "Oh, one other thing," I said. I pulled the envelope from my pocket and tossed it on his desk.

"What's this?" Fingers asked.

"My expenses," I said.

Fingers opened the envelope and flipped through the bills. He looked up at me. "I don't get it," he said. "These are untouched. Everything's intact."

"So's my conscience," I said and left.

I went down to the Garden Room to see if my stomach could take a little breakfast. I wasn't positive it could, but thought I'd try. I took a booth by myself, at the back, near the windows that opened to the garden area outside. The light was warm and made me feel almost whole. I ordered the poached eggs on toast, along with a cup of joe.

While I waited I pulled out the application Queeney had given me and started filling it out. Maybe he was right. If I was going to do this, why not do it properly? I was nearly halfway done when a vision of loveliness with long legs joined me in my booth. It suddenly smelled of lavender.

"You look terrible," Virginia said.

"At least I look better than I feel."

"I heard what happened," she said.

I didn't answer.

"What have you got there?" she asked, turning her head to read the paper.

"Application for a P.I. license," I said. "Queeney thinks I should go out on my own. Says I should cut ties completely."

"And what do you think?"

I looked into her brown eyes. "I think I'm a sap who

doesn't know what he wants until it's too late."

Virginia gave me a kind smile. "I won't argue with you there."

"I'm sorry," I said.

She reached across the table and took my hand. "I am too," she said.

I wasn't sure what she had to be sorry about, except maybe getting involved with a huckster like me. But it was a kind gesture.

"Were you sweet on her?" she asked.

I shook my head.

She kept my hand but fiddled with my thumb. "Did you..." she paused, then tried again. "Did you..."

"No," I said.

She nodded and looked down.

I reached over and lifted up her chin. "We kissed," I said. "Nothing more. I was a schoolboy flattered by the attention. Not understanding that she played me for a patsy and I was just the right dope to fall for it. I didn't mean to hurt you."

She tried a smile.

"Maybe we could start over," I offered.

She didn't answer.

The waitress brought my eggs. "Can I get you anything?" she asked Virginia.

"No," she said. "I'll just have some of his."

She slid over next to me. I smiled and pushed over the plate. "What are you doing Friday?" I asked. "There's a kid, plays the sax at the Moulin Rouge, supposed to be pretty good. Jimmy Five invited me."

She took a piece of toast and laid a poached egg on top. I watched her bring it up to her lips. "We'll see," she said and gave me a wink.

It was the best wink I'd ever gotten.

EPILOGUE

"WHERE ARE YOU taking me?"

The man in front of her turned and placed an arm over the seat of the car. His tailored suit slid up, revealing dark cufflinks and a monogram that read "S. M."

"Just a little place we know," he said.

"I'm not who you think I am."

The man grinned. "Oh, you're exactly who we think you are."

She turned to the large man sitting, arms folded, on the seat next to her. He eyeballed her but did not smile. She instinctively rubbed her arms, still able to feel the strength of his grip.

"You know," the man in the front seat said. "I'm a big fan of your work. Drugging Rossi like that to make it seem like an overdose was pure genius." He gave her a broad smile. "Course, I didn't tell the boss you'd done it to Rossi. But he'll find out soon enough."

The man turned and pointed toward a dirt road just ahead. "Take that left up there, Vito," he said to the driver.

She noticed her hand was shaking but couldn't stop it, so she slipped it under the coat across her lap. "Isn't there something we can work out, Mr...?"

The man turned again. "Manella," he said casually. "Salvatore Manella, but you can call me Sal."

She tried to smile. "Isn't there something we can work out, Sal? You're a handsome man."

"Oh no," he said. "I've seen what you do to men. Count me out."

The large man next to her chuckled.

The driver turned onto the dirt road. As large as the man was next to her, this one was even bigger, so much so that he had to remove his hat just to fit in the driver's seat. The car jerked and bumped with each rut in the road. The man hit his head on the car's ceiling several times. It didn't stop him. A pounding could be heard from the trunk. Or was it her heart?

A remorse took hold of her like a wet coat in a rainstorm. Why hadn't she just left? Why did she feel the need to take the detective out as well? What had he really done that was so bad? He'd rejected her, that's what. She'd thrown herself at him and he'd rejected her. Her face tightened. That was enough.

Her father's words came back to her. "Whatever you have to do, you do it. If somebody gets in the way, you take them out. You don't let anyone or anything stop you."

She didn't. Dorsey was becoming a problem, so she fixed it. The El Rancho dealer was cheating, so she fixed him too. They'd find his body in a couple of days. Rossi, however, had proven a formidable adversary. He was smart, and he paid attention. He saw her luggage in the suite that day, and while he had tried to hide it, tried to make up a foolish story about shoes, she knew he'd seen it.

But taking out Rossi had cost her. She could have let it go. She could have just left when that imbecile dealer called and told her Rossi knew about Dorsey. But how could she have known they'd be waiting for her right outside the suite? There must be something she could do.

"If you know about Rossi, then you must be from the Sands," she said. "We didn't even hit the Sands."

"Come now," the man named Sal said. "We both know that isn't true. You and that dealer were already pulling fast ones, seeing what you could get away with. You know that, and we know it too."

"I have money," she offered in desperation.

He just laughed at her.

She jumped forward, her arms flailing, slapping him about the head. The man next to her reached over, placed a hand on her chest, and flung her back against the seat. It pulled her breath away.

The man named Sal straightened his hair. "Is that really necessary?" he asked.

She sat in silence as the car rode on; the pounding in the trunk remained steady.

"Pull up over there," the man named Sal said to the driver.

When the car came to a stop, she watched him get out of the front seat. He adjusted his suit, shooting his cuffs. He seemed very particular about the way he dressed. She smiled at the thought of sand getting into his shoes. The driver got out as well, the car rocking with the strain of his weight.

"Out," the man next to her ordered. "No tricks."

She saw the butt of the gun sticking out of his waistband. It was a cross draw, meant to be pulled out with his right hand. The hand that was facing her.

"Go on," he said. "Get out."

Before he could move, she dove across the seat, throwing her shoulder into his right side, catching him off guard and pinning his arm. He groped clumsily for her with his left. She reached for his gun, just as the door on her side swung open and two hands took hold of her ankles, pulling her free from the car in one swift motion.

It was the driver.

She laid on the ground for a moment, trying to catch her breath, before standing. When she did, the man named Sal backhanded her, knocking her again to the ground.

The men moved to the back of the car and opened the trunk. They pulled out her accomplice, the Sands' dealer, and threw him to the ground. He had a gag in his mouth and was bound at the feet, his arms tied behind his back. He must have been kicking the car the entire way, hoping against hope that someone would hear.

She'd heard him.

"Cut him loose," the man named Sal ordered.

The driver pulled out a knife and cut the ropes that bound the dealer's legs and hands. The other man, the one who was sitting next to her, dug his fingers into her arm and yanked her up from the ground. She turned and kicked him square between the legs, as hard as she could. He dropped. That's when she heard the distinctive click.

"Go ahead," the man named Sal said. "See if you can outrun lead." He motioned to the driver with his head. The driver pulled the dealer away from the car and took him out into the desert. The gun ordered her to follow.

213

She did.

She had never spent much time in the desert. It wasn't anything like California. No trees, no greenery, no foliage, no water. Nothing but dirt and sand. She had always seen it as a lonely place. A barren place. But as she scanned the area, as she looked into the hazy heat rising in waves, she started to understand its beauty. The purple hue of the mountains as the sun settled in the west. The cactus and Joshua trees standing in defiance against a cruel and uncaring Mother Nature.

She thought of her father; everything he had shown her. Taught her. She'd never met her mother, but she always felt she knew her. Always felt close to her. Her father had described her so very well. She could see her mother's long brown hair bouncing on her shoulders. Her smile filling her face.

"You got it?" the man named Sal asked the driver.

The driver pulled a small gun from the pocket of his suit and handed it to him. It looked larger in his hand.

The man named Sal examined the gun. "This his?" he asked.

The driver nodded. "Took it from him myself," he said.

The man named Sal moved behind her. "Take this," he whispered in her ear and placed the gun in her hand. She took hold of it, squeezing her fingers around the wooden grip.

"Now, shoot the scumbag dealer who was stealing from our casino," he said. He placed the barrel of his own gun to her head and cocked the trigger. "Just the dealer," he added.

The driver stepped backward.

She raised the gun. She could see the fear in the dealer's eyes. Eyes that pleaded with her not to pull the trigger. She didn't listen.

There was a loud pop, and the dealer dropped to the ground.

"Whoa, ho, ho," the man named Sal exclaimed. "She didn't even hesitate. Oh, sister. I really like you."

She turned to face him. "Do you?" she asked.

"Oh yeah," he said and raised his gun. He held out his hand, palm up, and motioned for her to give him the gun.

She brought it to her head and looked him straight in the eyes. There was nothing there. No fear. No emotion. No remorse.

"That's too bad," she said and pulled the trigger.

ABOUT THE AUTOR

Paul W. Papa is a full-time writer and ghost writer who has lived in Las Vegas for more than thirty years. He developed a fascination with the area, and all its wonders, while working for nearly fifteen years at several Las Vegas casinos. In his role as a security officer, Paul was the person who actually shut and locked the doors of the Sands Hotel and Casino for the final time. He eventually became a hotel investigator for a major Strip casino, during which time he developed a love for writing stories about uncommon events. When not at his keyboard, Paul can be found talking to tourists on Fremont Street, investigating some old building, or sitting in a local diner hunting down his next story.

Rossi's Risk

Keep reading for a sneak preview of the next book in the Max Rossi Series. Rossi has to solve a murder by going into a part of town where he's definately not wanted.

Coming winter of 2020

ONE

THE PLACE HAD barely been open for a month. It was an experiment really. A test to see how it would do in a town that had often been labeled "the Mississippi of the West." It was called the Moulin Rouge, after the famed Parisian cabaret, birthplace of the raunchy dance known as the Cancan. It was to be the first interracial casino in Las Vegas—welcoming both whites and coloreds. We were headed there to see the Tropi Can Can revue, or more specifically, the young colored sax player who was making a name for himself as part of Benny Carter's band. Jimmy Five of the Five and Dimes arranged tickets to the show and we were to meet him and his gal Nancy Williams—a Dice Girl—at the casino.

Virginia made me wait three days before she agreed to go with me, a penance I was paying for having pressed my lips where they didn't belong. I'd seen the error of my ways and my Copa Girl had somehow managed to forgive me for the deed; or maybe she just wanted to see her show's competition. Of course, having almost died in the process helped.

I pulled my bright red Roadmaster into the porte cochère and was met by a colored valet attendant—the first of his kind in Las Vegas. I didn't mind. He took a piece of paper from his jacket pocket, tore it in half, and handed me one of the halves. Then he placed the other under my wiper blade, the same as the white valet attendants did at the Sands. I tossed him a couple of nuggets from my pocket.

I opened the passenger door and let out my leggy companion. She wore a light blue sheath dress with matching kitten heels and a white bolero jacket. Crystals dangled from each ear and a matching piece adorned her very lovely neck. Her gloves were white, her purse clutch, and her eyes brown. Her brunette locks were parted to the side, sweeping behind her right ear and cascading down her left side in an abundance of curls. She was simply marvelous and I told her so.

She kissed me on the cheek and my knees buckled a bit.

Other than the name, Las Vegas' version of the French landmark looked nothing like its Paris counterpart. The front was demure, except for the larger than life, googie-style lettering, designed by neon sign artist Betty Willis, that rested atop the main building. The same words accompanied a 60-foot high neon Eiffel Tower, which was also designed by Willis. I thought it strange that there wasn't a red windmill in sight.

The original Moulin Rouge burned down some thirty years ago. I hoped Will Max Schwartz's version fared better.

I gave Virginia my arm, and she took it. A hint of lavender filled the air as we headed inside. We were greeted by a colored doorman who opened the door just fine for us as we entered. I handed him another couple of nuggets.

Inside, the "Resort Wonder of the World," as it was booked, resembled every other casino in town: dim lights, busy carpets, no windows or clocks, the distinct sound of coins dropping into metal trays. There was, of course, one exception: the place was filled with people of all shades and colors. They were dressed to the nines and there were a lot of them. All enjoying themselves, gambling, drinking, and having a good time. Just like every other casino.

We found Jimmy and Nancy near the entrance to the theater, talking to a large man with a cauliflower ear. I recognized him right away.

Jimmy lit up when he saw us. "Hey, glad you two could make it," he said.

We shook hands. Virginia leaned in and rubbed cheeks with Nancy. I kept my distance.

Jimmy turned to the man standing next to him. "This is..."

"Joe Louis," I said, finishing his sentence. "The Brown Bomber. I am very pleased to meet you."

The boxer held out his hand. It dwarfed mine, but I took it anyway. It was firm, but light, as if he was intentionally holding back. Like how a giant might shake hands with a child. Joe Louis was an idol of mine. I'd done a little boxing back in Boston. My father thought I should be able to defend myself and took me to a gym. It was a good gym, and I learned quite a bit about the sport of pugilism. Even had a couple fights of my own.

"Joe's part owner of the Moulin Rouge," Jimmy offered.

The big man tried a smile, but it didn't work. There was something melancholy about him. He had one of those faces that always appeared to be holding a secret—a painful secret, something he wanted to share, but knew he couldn't. He became the heavyweight champion on June 22, 1937, when he knocked out James J. Braddock in eight rounds. My father had taken me to Chicago to see the fight. I was just a young kid, but the man had an impact on me.

"I watched you fight in '37," I said. "Saw you knock out Braddock in eight and Schmeling in one."

The side of the man's mouth raised. It was probably as close to a true smile as he ever got. "That was some fight," he admitted.

I assumed he was referring to the Schmeling fight. Having lost to the man in '36, Louis would never consider himself a true champion and until he beat the German-born Schmeling—something he did handily, much to Hitler's chagrin.

"You a fighter?" he asked.

"I've dabbled," I said.

"You ought to come to Johnny Tocco's," he offered. "Show us what you got."

My mouth formed a silly grin, like a kid who'd just been offered a pony. "I'd like that," I said.

He told me to come by anytime, then excused himself, turning to the line that was forming behind him. We headed into the showroom and were taken to our seats. The ladies seemed impressed, especially with the stage. I didn't blame them. The room was larger than I expected it to be. Complete with a full stage that rivaled the Copa Room and huge, draping curtains. Tables, some round, some square, were set in rows. The back wall was decorated with a painting of fancy women, dancing the Cancan on the streets of France, a large windmill in the background. It was the first place I saw one.

We'd missed the dinner show—both ladies had dancing to do—but were just in time for the 2:30 am late show—or early show, depending how you looked at it.

Jimmy had done very well, getting us seats in the front, adjacent to the band where we could easily hear the sax player.

A cocktail waitress came to our seats and we ordered our two-drink minimums. The ladies each chose a tom collins, Jimmy a sloe gin fizz, and I my typical manhattan. The room filled quickly and there were just as many white people as anyone else. As the band began to play, the stage came alive with colored dancers in bright, pleated dresses, scandalously lifting their garter-clad legs high in the air, revealing their ruffled drawers. Plumed hats strapped to their heads.

The music was fast paced, as was the dancing. And just as Jimmy had implied, the kid on the alto saxophone stood out. He was young, dressed in the suit coat and tie that was the band's uniform. As he played, I began to direct my attention away from the dancers toward him. His fingers flew effortlessly on the keys and he played long stretches with little breath. I was both mesmerized and impressed.

The dancers were about halfway into their routine, when the doors at the back of the room flung open, and bluebottles came pouring in. O'Malley, a detective I had history with, was at the lead. The music stopped, as did the dancing, and all heads turned. O'Malley and several of the bluebottles headed directly to the band. He stood right in front of the sax player.

The man's eyes widened.

Moses Jones," O'Malley said. "You're under arrest for the murder of Margaret Lee Paige."

One of the dancers fainted.

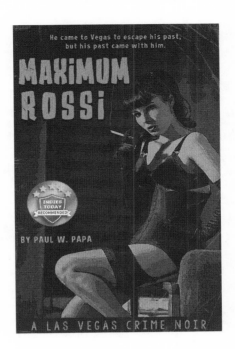

He came to Vegas to escape his past, but his past came with him.

MAXIMUM ROSSI

BY PAUL W. PAPA

A LAS VEGAS CRIME NOIR

PRAISE FOR MAXIMUM ROSSI

"To find a modern pastiche of the noir/hardboiled novels of the 40s and 50s this good is quite rare. This is a really decent homage to the age of Chandler and Hammett, and it's a pleasure to read." - **Booksplainer**

"A wildly pleasurable and perfectly written gritty crime drama." - **Indies Today**

"This is an excellent hard-boiled mystery: cleverly written, smoothly paced, and with a protagonist who's compelling enough to sustain a series." - **Publisher's Weekly**

"A companionable mob tale, enjoyable unserious and dramatically immersive." - **Kirkus Reviews**

DON'T MISS OUT!

To keep up with Max's adventures.

Sign up for Paul W. Papa's newsletter at:

https://mailchi.mp/8be9ac154607/paulwpapa

To find out inside facts and tidbits about the Sands, Las Vegas, and Rossi's world, join *The Adventures of Max Rossi* Facebook group at:

www.facebook.com/groups/623467625095507/

You can find out more about Paul W. Papa

on his Facebook page at:

www.facebook.com/PaulWPapa/

or on his website at:

www.paulwpapa.com/

If you enjoyed this book, please leave a review on Amazon. Reviews help authors get noticed.

Made in the USA
Middletown, DE
08 July 2021